the one that GOT away

KERIS STAINTON

Bookouture

Published by Bookouture in 2018

An imprint of StoryFire Ltd.

Carmelite House
50 Victoria Embankment
London EC4Y 0DZ

www.bookouture.com

ISBN: 978-1-78681-455-5
eBook ISBN: 978-1-78681-454-8

Previously published as *The Invitation*

the
one
that
GOT
away

ALSO BY KERIS STAINTON

WOMEN'S FICTION
If You Could See Me Now
It Had to be You

CHILDREN'S AND YA
One Italian Summer
Lily and the Christmas Wish
Counting Stars
Spotlight on Sunny
Starring Kitty
Baby, One More Time (as Esme Taylor)
All I Want for Christmas (as Esme Taylor)
Emma Hearts LA
Jessie Hearts NYC
Della Says: OMG!

NON-FICTION
Happy Home Ed
Calm Like a Stupid Feather
As Delightful as a Carrot

For Jenni Nock, hope I did him justice

CHAPTER ONE

Piper held her phone at arms' length and about a foot above her head to get the best angle and include as much of her outfit as possible. She was wearing a red and white striped long-sleeved T-shirt and black dungarees with gold glitter ankle boots and she was totally feeling herself. Apart from one thing.

Sweaty with nerves/excitement she typed. *Catch me on Hey, UK! at 9.30 talking about body positivity*

She posted the photo to her Instagram, waited a second for a couple of likes and then shut her phone down before shoving it in the internal pocket of her satchel. She glanced around the room. The TV chef who'd been on earlier demonstrating from his new book of pies 'for real men' was still sitting in the corner, talking quietly on his phone. Piper had wanted to try the bacon and black pudding pie he'd made, but a) she was too nervous to eat, and b) she wasn't a real man.

She sipped at her water and glanced at the large flat-screen TV. 9.10. Only twenty minutes until she was going to be on national TV. She hoped her friends were watching. She knew her friends would be watching. And quite a lot of her IG followers – she'd been getting messages steadily since she'd first mentioned it a couple of days earlier. She doubted any family would be tuning in since a) her parents were dead, b) her aunt didn't tend to get up before ten and c) her sister hadn't seemed at all interested when she'd told her about it.

She took her phone out and switched it on again, chewing her mouth a little before remembering the bold lip the make-up

artist had given her earlier. Once her phone had powered up, she
checked her face in the front camera. All good. Well, she looked
nervous – eyes wide and too bright – but her lippie looked great.
She opened Twitter and typed *On in fifteen. Want to do the Power
Pose, but I think it would freak out Pie Guy.*

Pie Guy glanced up briefly – his bright blue eyes meeting
Piper's. He was quite hot, she thought. She'd noticed he had really
nice hands when she'd watched him baking on the big screen.
But she couldn't go out with anyone who thought pies were just
for men. And she'd seen his girlfriend on the sidebar of shame
and she was about the size of one of Piper's thighs. She shut her
phone down again – she was absolutely going to leave it this
time – and anxiously wiped her sweaty hands on her dungarees.

'Don't be nervous,' the man said.

Piper laughed. 'Easy for you to say. This is my first time.'

He looked up then, one eyebrow curving. 'Virgin, eh?'

'Ugh,' Piper said, before she could stop herself.

He laughed. 'Sorry. But seriously. You'll be fine. Susannah's
lovely. I've done this show loads.'

Piper nodded. She'd been briefly introduced to Susannah when
she'd arrived and she was definitely lovely. Warm, friendly, with
glossy chocolate brown hair flowing over her narrow shoulders
and a pair of black-rimmed glasses perched on the end of her
nose. It wasn't Susannah Piper was worried about: it was the
woman she'd been invited on to debate with. Naomi Jones.
Piper had seen her byline photo – a short blonde bob, bright
pink lipstick, over-plucked eyebrows. She looked friendly with
a hint of intimidating, like a primary school head teacher. The
researcher Piper had spoken to on the phone had insisted Naomi
was lovely and not interested in an argument, but Piper wasn't
sure, mostly because a) Naomi hadn't sounded at all lovely in the
article she'd written, and b) Piper had watched this show before
and they always seemed to be interested in an argument.

She shuffled forward on the squashy sofa and poured herself another glass of water from the jug on the coffee table. Her mouth was so dry that when she'd tried to introduce herself to the researcher, she'd actually blown a spit bubble. So that had been an excellent start. The researcher had either not noticed or pretended not to notice to be kind. Piper gulped the water down and then took a few what she hoped were relaxing breaths. In, two, three. Out, two, three. She couldn't believe she'd actually agreed to do this.

'All okay in here?' the researcher – Piper thought her name was Julia? Or Julianne? –said, popping her head round the door. 'Need anything?'

'Thanks,' Piper said. 'I'm good.' She needed the loo, but she knew she probably didn't really. It was just nervous wee. And she was wearing dungarees so she wasn't going to chance it anyway.

The door closed and opened again and Naomi Jones walked in. She was dressed a lot more smartly than Piper in a navy blue shirt dress with a string of red beads around her neck and bright red ballerina flats. She looked a bit like a Tory wife. Or the presenter of a homes show on Channel 5.

'Hello!' she said, crossing the room directly towards Piper, her hand already outstretched. 'I'm Naomi.'

Piper stood up and clasped Naomi's hand, making sure to make eye contact and keep smiling. 'I'm Piper,' she said. 'Nice to meet you.'

'You too!' Naomi said, sitting on the edge of the other sofa. 'Thanks so much for doing this.'

'No problem,' Piper said, as if Naomi had arranged the whole thing and Piper was her reluctant guest. 'I'm looking forward to it.'

'Me too,' Naomi replied. She poured herself a glass of water, but then held the glass on her knee without drinking any. 'Have you been on before?'

Piper shook her head. 'I haven't done any TV before.'

Naomi's eyes widened. 'Wow. In at the deep end then!'

Piper nodded. 'Feels that way, yeah.'

'I think this is my...' Naomi scrunched up her nose in thought. 'Fifth time? Maybe? I sometimes get it confused with *This Morning*.'

Piper smiled. She refused to be intimidated. *This Morning*. Big whoop. She sipped more water and looked over Naomi's head at the TV screen. They were due on in fifteen minutes. Her stomach swooped with nerves.

'I'm just going to pop to the loo.'

She peed, even though she didn't need to pee, and washed her hands while staring at herself in the mirror. She looked good. Her hair was behaving today – her fringe not doing that flicky-up thing that drove her mad. Her lipstick was really working for her. She grinned at herself, checking her teeth. And then she put her hands on her hips, pushed her chest out, and did the Power Pose she'd seen online. She looked good. She felt good. She was going to rock the shit out of this debate.

CHAPTER TWO

'That went well, I thought,' Naomi said, as the two of them were ushered back into the green room.

Piper felt a bit shell-shocked. It had all gone by in a bit of a blur. They'd been seated at a table in the mocked-up kitchen that was part of the show's set. She'd been able to see the live feed on an enormous flat screen TV on the wall, which she'd found really distracting – she'd kept glancing at it and catching her own eye. The presenter had clasped their hands and introduced herself before scanning her notes and then launching into the interview with few preliminaries. Piper had expected a chat maybe? Or some sort of dry run. But no, it all just… happened. Live.

Piper wasn't even sure what she'd said. She remembered waiting for Naomi to finish talking about people being responsible for their own health, mentally rehearsing her response that no one had the right to demand anyone's health, that health wasn't a moral imperative, that plenty of people did things that negatively impacted their own health and weren't demonised for it like fat people were. But she wasn't sure if she'd actually said any of that or if it had all stayed in her head.

Naomi picked up her bag, shrugged on her jacket and headed out, calling 'Bye' over her shoulder. Piper sat down on the sofa and poured herself a glass of water. The green room was empty now – she could see the chef on the flat-screen TV doing his next segment in the fake kitchen. She switched her phone back on and flinched as it started to chime and buzz in her hand. She felt absolutely exhausted, her neck and shoulders tight with stress.

'Piper?' One of the researchers was standing in the doorway. 'Are you ready to go?'

'Umm…' Piper took another swig of water, checked that she had everything – phone, bag, jacket – and stood up. 'I guess.'

'Well done,' the researcher said, as she showed Piper through the office and towards the main doors.

'Thanks,' Piper said. 'I don't really remember much about it.'

'You did very well.'

She opened the door, smiled brightly at Piper and then closed it behind her, leaving Piper standing on a busy London street, at ten in the morning, feeling like she'd just woken up from a stress dream. She forced herself to take a few slow breaths before crossing the road and heading up towards the Tube. The smell of bacon drifted out of a nearby cafe and Piper's stomach rumbled. Breakfast was a good idea. Breakfast and a coffee and then work. As soon as she was inside the cafe – a hipster-looking place with bare brick walls and industrial metal tables outside – all she wanted was to sit down and phone… well, she wanted to phone her mum, but that wasn't an option.

Instead, she called her sister.

'Did you watch?' she asked before either of them had even said hello.

'I saw it,' Holly said.

Piper could tell immediately that her sister was at the gym, probably on a treadmill. She'd spoken to her sister at the gym often enough that she recognised the echo.

'I'm at the gym and it was on the screen, but no sound. The subtitles were on, but they weren't great. It looked good though. I like that lipstick on you.'

'So I didn't disgrace myself?' Piper asked, against her better judgement.

'Not as far as I could tell! But like I said, I didn't watch it properly. It'll be online by the time I get home, right?'

'I would think so, yeah.'

'Are you on your way to work now?'

'Just getting breakfast. I've got the morning off.'

'Cool. Talk later when I've watched it then.'

'Great.'

Piper put her phone down on the table, ignoring all her notifications. Coffee. She needed coffee. She ordered a latte with an extra shot and eggs Benedict, and only then looked at her texts. Silver from work had sent her a series of thumbs up and smiley face emojis. Matt, her BFF, had sent a picture of himself watching the TV with 'proud of you' scrawled across it. All of the texts were positive, which Piper had pretty much expected. Her friend Alice wrote, 'You are an inspiration'. She kept scrolling back until she got to one from Matt that she'd missed just before she show. It just said 'Wreck her.' Piper laughed. Her friends were so great. But she felt sort of… hollow. Breakfast would help.

'You were good,' the waiter said as he put her eggs Benedict down on the table.

'What?' Piper blinked up at him. He was hot too – black beard speckled with silver, bedhead that she knew he probably spent at least twenty minutes and a tenner's worth of product creating in the morning, bright blue eyes.

'On the breakfast show.' He pointed at a screen on the wall behind the counter. Piper hadn't noticed.

'Oh shit,' she breathed.

He grinned. 'No. You were great. Held your own against that snotty cow.'

Piper looked down at her breakfast and then back up at him, smiling. 'Thank you. She was okay really. Not exactly friendly.'

'No,' he said. 'And you were right anyway. As long as you're healthy, eh?'

'Um,' Piper said. 'Yeah. Kind of.'

'I'll leave you to get on with it. Let me know if you need anything.' He stared at Piper for a second too long and she wondered if he was flirting.

'Thanks,' she said, and picked up her knife and fork.

She watched him walk back behind the counter and wondered if someone else – Silver or Matt – would have asked him out. Or not even asked him out, just done something with an eyebrow that meant 'meet me in the bathroom'. Piper had never been good at that sort of thing, never really believed someone was into her until they actually told her in so many words. She felt a pang of embarrassment, remembering a photographer at the work Christmas party, one hand down the front of her dress, mouth attached to her neck, and a voice in her head saying 'Does he like me though?' She'd laughed at the time, it had been so ridiculous, and he'd murmured, 'You like that, baby?' directly into her ear, which had only made her laugh more. And he'd kissed her to shut her up.

*

Piper didn't look at the rest of her social media until lunch. The couple of people at work who had seen the show had been complimentary and her boss, John, had watched it online in his office mid-morning and then popped his head round the door to tell her she'd done really well. No one so far had mentioned the subject that she'd been on to discuss, which she thought was kind of interesting. But she also suspected Twitter would have that aspect covered, which was why she'd waited so long to have a look. She blinked when she saw her notifications. The first few she read were positive. Then there were a few along the lines of she'd done great and that she was sexier and clearly healthier than the 'skinny bitch' she'd been debating. Piper rolled her eyes – these people literally thought they were criticising fat shaming by body shaming someone else. How could they not get that? There were a couple from men telling her they still found her attractive even though she was fat and some asking her to follow them – so they could grace her DMs with dick pics, no doubt. She blocked a couple of them, muted some more, but all in all – and to her surprise – the positive definitely outweighed the negative.

Her Instagram was the usual mix of lovely, supportive comments, and people who seemed to assume she didn't know she was fat. Someone literally posted 'Fat' on every single picture she ever put up. She'd wondered if they did it all over the internet, commenting 'Food' on recipes and 'Tweet' on Twitter. What an odd way to behave.

Facebook was better since her account was locked down and the comments from friends were all positive. She ignored the Messenger tab where she suspected some strangers' opinions – and, most likely, penises – lingered. They could wait for later.

She spent the afternoon amending a contract for a new girl band the company was hoping to sign. She hadn't seen them yet – or heard their music – but the A&R department was very excited and John had told her to ignore everything else in her in-tray and focus on getting this done. They were called Feminine Hygiene and an email had gone round asking everyone to try to come up with a new 'less confrontational' name. Piper's boss had suggested Feminine Hijinks, which had made Piper cry laughing, but none of the other suggestions were much better: The Muffin Tops; The Manicures; Dolly.

Piper was desperate to come up with something that wasn't actively offensive, but she hadn't managed it so far.

CHAPTER THREE

'Hey, sexy lady!' Matt called out as Piper walked out of the main gates of the building.

She grinned at him. 'Damn, they're meant to remove pervs from the premises. Don't know why they made us all chip in for that water cannon if they're not going to use it.'

As soon as she reached him, she wrapped her arms around his waist and squeezed.

'You okay?' he said into the top of her head.

'Tired.'

'You were brilliant this morning, babe.'

He'd already texted to tell her this, but she was happy to hear it again.

'Thanks.'

'Had any shitty comments?'

'Couple.' She let him go so they could start walking up to the pub. 'Few pervs. Some people telling me I'm fat.'

Matt mock-gasped. 'Shit! I'm sorry. Didn't you know? I'm a terrible friend.'

She laughed. 'I know, right? All these years and you never mentioned it.'

Matt had been fat when they met at university. Piper and Matt had gravitated together – both Northern, both quite loud, but not as confident as they pretended to be. They'd become BFFs ridiculously quickly, inseparable within a couple of weeks.

They'd kissed once at a New Year's Eve party. Matt had smoked then and Piper was always trying to bum cigarettes from him, even though she'd never smoked in her life. That night, he'd let her. He'd put the cig between her lips and cupped his hand around her mouth to light it. She hadn't even had time to inhale when he'd taken it back out again and pressed his lips to hers. She'd been sort of startled, but also drunk enough to decide to just go with it. It hadn't been a good kiss. They'd had zero chemistry. He'd pulled away, mumbled 'sorry', put the cig back in her mouth and they hadn't mentioned it for years. Not long after, Matt had started going out with Joe, a boy on their course, who wore a leather jacket, hardly ever turned up to lectures and acted as if Matt didn't exist. Matt had been completely besotted.

Another drunken night, Matt had told Piper he was bi. Now he was seeing Rebecca, who was sweet and funny and way more into Matt than he was into her. It was a pattern. Piper was so grateful she'd never been interested in him romantically; she'd totally have got her heart broken.

They walked around the corner and crossed the road into the pub they always went to when Matt met Piper from work, which he tried to do at least once a week. It wasn't the kind of pub Matt preferred –it was dark and dingy and favoured by locals, whereas Matt usually liked hipster bars with imported beers and fancy nibbles – but they'd popped in once and kept coming back ever since. The staff knew them now, they had their favourite table in the bay window and Matt even allowed himself a packet of Scampi Fries, which Piper had been sworn to secrecy about.

'How's Becks?' Piper asked, once they were seated – Piper with a bottle of Corona, Matt with a gin and tonic, and the pack of pungent-smelling crisps pulled open on the table between them.

'She's good,' Matt said, nodding. 'Haven't seen her for a few days.'

'Oh god. Are you dumping her?'

Matt picked up a crisp and popped it in his mouth. 'Maybe.'

'Matt! Why?'

He shrugged. 'I don't know. She's great. She's just not... I don't look forward to seeing her. I mean, we have fun, yeah? But I was more excited just now waiting to see you than I am when I see her.'

'Well,' Piper said, picking up her drink. 'That's cos I'm awesome.'

'You are.' Matt grinned. 'You were so great this morning. I was so proud of you.'

She smiled at him. One of the things she'd loved the most when she first met him was how open he was about his feelings. He'd told her he loved her within a few weeks, and was always effusive with his praise and his emotions. She'd struggled a bit at first (she'd said 'Me... um... too' when he'd said 'I love you' and he still took the piss about it occasionally), but now it was easier. They always said they loved each other when they ended a phone call; it came naturally to Piper now.

'Have you read all your messages yet?' Matt asked.

The pub door opened and they were hit with a blast of cold air. Matt shivered dramatically.

'Not yet,' Piper said. 'I had some on Facebook, but—'

But the thought of reading them had made her feel like a teenager again, standing outside a party and hearing her friends talking about what a mess she looked that night. She didn't want to say that to Matt.

'Have a look now then. If they're terrible, we can get hammered.'

Piper knew Matt couldn't actually get hammered – he had to be up for work at six in the morning – but it was a sweet offer.

'Fine,' Piper said. She took a fortifying swig of her beer and tapped open Messenger. The messages from her friends were all lovely, of course, but she had a bunch of notifications from strangers too.

'This guy wants to motorboat me,' Piper said, pinching a Scampi Fry.

'That seems fair enough,' Matt said. 'You do have magnificent bosoms. Block him.'

Piper blocked him. The next message was supportive and funny – from a woman saying she agreed with everything Piper said and asking where she'd got her lipstick. Piper thanked her and sent her links both to the lipstick and her Instagram. The next one said *I used to be like you. I was unhappy and comfort eating and I didn't have the energy to exercise* and then tried to get her to sign up to some aloe vera pyramid scheme thing. Piper blocked her. There were a few more letting her know she was fat. 'Do they think I don't know?' she asked Matt. 'It's literally what I was on there to talk about.' And a couple telling her she'd never get a man looking the way she did, which she knew wasn't true and didn't care about anyway. And then, towards the end, there was—

'No,' Piper said, putting her phone down on the table and picking up her beer.

'What?' Matt asked. 'If it's another dickhead just get 'em blocked.'

'No,' Piper said again. 'It's not… It's—' She picked her phone back up and held it out so Matt could see the screen.

'Ho-lee shit,' Matt said, squinting. 'Is that—'

'Yeah.'

Piper's hands were shaking. She put her phone down on the table again and pushed her hands under her thighs. Rob. Rob Kingsford. He'd been 'Kingy' for a while at school. And then 'Robbie'. And then, eventually, 'Rob'. Piper hadn't heard from him since she'd moved to London. And she hadn't even stalked his Facebook for ages. Months, probably. Definitely weeks.

'What does he want?' Matt asked.

'I don't know,' Piper said. 'I can't look.'

Piper picked up her phone again and stared at Rob's photo. He looked basically the same as he had done at school, except obviously older and bigger. In her head, he was still so much the

Rob from school that the picture almost looked like Rob's hotter older brother. She couldn't quite imagine what this version of Rob would be like in real life. She knew, from her Facebook stalking, that he was a runner – he'd done the Manchester Run and even some sort of mini Iron Man, plus the mud thing everyone seemed to do at least once and which looked like Piper's worst nightmare.

'Jesus, are you drooling?' Matt asked. 'Give it here, I'll read it.'

'No,' Piper said. 'I can…' But she couldn't.

Matt reached for the phone and Piper let him take it.

'Hi,' he read.

Piper closed her eyes and gripped the edge of the table.

'Saw you on TV this morning and just wanted to say you were completely brilliant. Is it weird to say I'm proud of you when we haven't been in touch all this time? Hope not. Too late now. Anyway. Hope things are really good with you. Would be great to catch up if you're ever home. Do you ever get home? Rob x'

'There's a kiss?' Piper asked, opening her eyes and leaning over to look at the phone. 'Really?'

'Jesus, woman, you're nearly thirty,' Matt said, sliding her phone back along the table.

'I'm twenty-fucking-six,' Piper said. She looked at the screen, but Matt had tapped out of Facebook.

'Yes, there was really a kiss,' Matt said. He put on a stupid voice: 'Do you think that means he likes you?'

'I just can't believe he messaged me,' Piper said.

'You haven't heard from him since school, right?'

'He sent a card when Mum and Dad…' She wafted her hand. 'But that's all. I've almost added him on Facebook so many times—'

'While stalking.'

'Yeah. Like… what's the harm? We were definitely friends. You can add friends on Facebook.'

'That's literally what it's for.'

'Yeah. But I always thought it would be weird. After all this time.'

'Apparently not,' Matt said. 'Since he messaged you. Check if he's added you.'

'Shit,' Piper said, tapping Facebook open again. She hadn't even thought of that. And there it was. A friend request from Rob Kingsford. Fuck.

'Accept it, you daft cow,' Matt said, reaching for the phone again.

'I can do it myself,' Piper said. And tapped.

'Now check his profile. See if he's single.

Piper shook her head, but she was already on it. 'No relationship info to show' she read. 'That doesn't mean he's not in a relationship...'

'You can check his photos for girlfriends later,' Matt said. 'I'm going to get us another drink. You want a gin?'

'No, I'll have another Corona.' Matt stood up and Piper grabbed his sleeve. 'Actually I'll have a gin, yeah. Thanks.'

Matt ducked down and kissed the top of her head before taking the two steps over to the bar.

Piper stared at the phone until dots danced in front of her eyes. Rob Kingsford. Rob Kingsford had messaged her. And added her. And suggested they meet up next time she was home. She had no plans to go home, but that wasn't the point. He wanted to see her. He'd thought about her.

'Now put your phone down and listen to me. I need to tell you what happened to Crazy Jay last night.'

Piper turned her phone face down, but as Matt talked about Jay – one of his colleagues who always seemed to get himself into utterly ridiculous, borderline illegal, situations – she let her mind drift back to Rob. At school. In the park. On the beach. The first time they met, he was up a tree. She heard his voice first and then looked up and saw his face peeking out from between the branches. And then his arms as he swung down and landed on the grass just in front of her.

'What an entrance,' he'd said. And she'd laughed. And that had been it: they'd been friends. There was a group of them who hung out on the prom and the beach and by the lake in the park in good weather, and sat in the shelters at the front of the park whenever it rained. When they got a bit older and a couple of them had Saturday jobs, they met in one of the numerous coffee shops on the high street. And then, even later, in Wetherspoons. Those nights – all of them talking and laughing in 'Spoons, before getting chips on the way home – were some of Piper's favourite memories. She didn't let herself think about it much. Sometimes, when she was trying to sleep, she couldn't help herself: they crept into her subconscious like smoke around a door. Rob smiling at her over the top of his pint, her knee pressing against his under the table. Claire sitting in his lap, her hand playing with the sagging collar of his T-shirt, her smile smug.

'Are you listening at all?' Matt said and Piper jumped.

'Shit. Sorry. No.'

'Talk about a face journey,' Matt said, doing an impression of Piper's face going from soft to angry to sad and confused.

'I was thinking about Rob,' she said.

'I assumed. So?'

'So?'

'So reply. Tell him you'll go out for a drink next time you're home.'

Piper shook her head. 'I don't think so. I think the past is best left in the past.'

CHAPTER FOUR

When Piper got to work the following morning, she found a printed memo on her desk with 'IMPORTANT' in red letters on the front page.

'The fuck is this?' she muttered, shrugging her coat off and hanging it over the back of her seat. There'd been some whispers that the company was in trouble and she really hoped this wasn't confirmation. She made a little money from her blog, but not enough to live on; it really just kept her in takeaways and the occasional Joanie dress.

As I'm sure you're all aware – the memo read –*we've recently signed a girl band that we're very excited about. They're fresh and funky and we're confident we'll be able to position them in direct competition with Little Mix. They're currently working with choreographers, stylists and producers, but in the meantime we need to come up with the perfect name.*

They came to us calling themselves Feminine Hygiene, which we're sure you'll all agree is not ideal for the target market. We've workshopped a few names ourselves, but we're not 100% on any of them. We'd love for everyone to get involved. We feel that not only will it give us access to a wide range of creative ideas, but also give everyone a sense of ownership over the band, which can only be positive going forward.

Piper rolled her eyes. Who had written this shit?

We've included a short list of names below, but this is in no way
to be considered a shortlist. Any and all suggestions are welcome.
There are no stupid ideas!
All Things Nice
Friend Zone (or Friendzone)
Six Inch Heels
Minxy

'Minxy?!' Piper said aloud before she could stop herself and
heard a resulting laugh from further down the office in Accounts.
And 'Friendzone' was definitely a stupid idea.

Vinylla
Big Hair Don't Care
Risky
Trigger Warning
Honey Badger

Grabbing a pen, she crossed out out all of the names apart from
'Risky' and wrote 'Best of a bad lot' next to it. Next to 'Honey
Badger', she wrote, 'This is what female Men's Rights Activists call
themselves so definitely out.' She closed her eyes and tapped the
pen against her teeth while she tried to think. 'Flower'? There must
surely already be a band named Flower. She wrote it down anyway;
it could be a jumping off point. She googled 'flower list' and scrolled
through, writing down any that had potential: Clover. Daisy. Peony.

*

She texted Matt. *Need a name for a girl band.*

He replied instantly. *Flaps. Brazilian Wax. Thigh Gap.*

SERIOUSLY Piper replied.

Sorry. My Starbucks Lovers. Smooch. The Maybes.

God Piper replied. *If I suggest Smooch, I bet they'll love it.*

The band or the bigwigs?

Bigwigs. The band called themselves Feminine Hygiene

Matt replied with a series of laugh/cry emojis and *I love them already.*

*

Piper set her phone down on the desk and pinned the memo up on the board next to her. It would actually be pretty cool to come up with the name they gave the band. And even cooler to prevent them from being called something gross like 'Smooch' or 'All Things Nice'.

She didn't want to stay in Legal forever. It was fine – it paid pretty well and her colleagues were great and the work was interesting – but repetitive. The problem was that she was too good at it and she'd made herself indispensable. John got into a flap whenever she took any time off, insisting that the temp replacements were worse than useless.

The problem was, Piper didn't know exactly what she did want to do. When things weren't quite as busy she liked to go and hang around the other departments a little, asking questions and trying to get to grips with exactly what they did. She thought Press might be an interesting fit. Or International – that way she'd get to travel – but she hadn't been brave enough to actually do anything about it yet. One day. Maybe.

She scrolled quickly through her emails, looking for anything that seemed important or urgent, but it was mostly standard stuff: people chasing contracts and invoice requisitions, producers looking to clear music samples, inter-office nonsense about the cleanliness (or otherwise) of the kitchen. She actually scrolled past the one unusual message, but something about it caught her eye as it disappeared off the top of the screen and she scrolled back up.

The subject line said *You should be ashamed!*

Piper's stomach was already churning when she clicked on it. It started 'Dear Fat Bitch' and then told her how disgusting she was, how they couldn't believe she'd even dared go on TV looking like she did. How dare she promote obesity when people were dying? And how much better Naomi had been than her. 'You need help' it ended.

Piper had received quite a few similar messages over the years. But not to her work email. Hands shaking, she double-checked it hadn't been forwarded from her Gmail or something, but no, it was direct.

She archived it and then immediately unarchived it – she should probably keep it somewhere, in case something happened. Or maybe she should reply and tell him to get fucked. No, she definitely shouldn't reply. She starred it so it would be easier to find and archived it again, then headed to the kitchen to make herself a tea.

'I saw you on TV yesterday,' Lee, one of her colleagues, said. He was just finishing making his coffee, stirring the mug and then dropping the teaspoon in the sink. 'You were good.'

'Thanks. It's all a bit of a blur now.'

'You haven't watched it back?'

Piper shook her head and faked a shudder. 'God no.'

'You should. You looked good.'

'Um,' Piper said. 'Thanks.'

Was he flirting? She didn't think he'd ever flirted with her before.

Lee leaned backwards out of the kitchen and looked behind him, then said, 'Actually, I've been wanting to ask you something?'

'Yeah?'

He drank some of his coffee and then said, 'Yeah. I was wondering if... um. Would you want to go and get a drink some time? After work maybe?'

Piper hadn't seen that coming. At all. But Lee seemed nice enough and it had been a while since she'd been on a date. And Matt always said that even bad dates were good practice, so. 'Yeah, actually. That sounds nice.'

Lee smiled. He wasn't great-looking – he had a bit of a monobrow going on and a shaving rash across his jaw – but he looked a lot better when he smiled.

'I can't do this week,' he said. 'I've got gigs every night. But how's next Monday?'

'Sounds good,' Piper said.

He left and she finished making her tea, taking it back to her desk and sitting down to stare at her screen again. She wasn't shaking any more. And she actually felt fine. It probably wasn't difficult to find her work email online; someone just had to have too much time on their hands and access to Google and that described plenty of people. And she'd got way more positive than negative messages this time, which she appreciated. Something definitely seemed to be changing since she'd started blogging. Although the worry was that it was all just a trend – body positivity was having a moment –and that things would eventually go back to how they'd been before.

She spent the morning working on amendments for a contract, had lunch sitting on a bench looking out over the river listening to a podcast, and picked up some prawns and a loaf of fresh bread on the way home.

Matt wasn't home – he usually got back about an hour after she did – so she showered and changed into her favourite pyjamas before pouring herself a glass of wine, cutting off a chunk of cheese and curling up on the sofa to watch an episode of *The Crown* on Netflix. Perfect.

CHAPTER FIVE

Piper had always intended to move to London for university. But she'd assumed she'd be going home to New Brighton, to her family, every holiday and possibly additional weekends. She'd only been in London for five months when her parents had died. And that had changed everything.

She'd gone home for a while. Just until she'd felt like she could stand without staggering. Could speak without weeping. Could breathe without it escaping through the gaping hole where her heart had been. She'd actually returned to London a little before she was ready. Because she'd been terrified that she'd never be ready and she'd stay at home – with Connie and Holly, who had still been living in New Brighton and working in Liverpool – and never get back to her own life.

*

Back in London, she threw herself into university, into student life, and tried to forget everything else. If she worked hard enough, if she went out enough, if she drank enough, she didn't have to think about the fact that her parents were never coming back. Ever.

She lived in Halls off Charlotte Street, which would have been a perfect introduction if the Halls hadn't been so shitty, but living in the centre of town had been exciting. Her friends all went out a lot, even though no one really had any money. They'd get £1 slices of pizza and cheap beer and either spend their nights in dingy clubs (everyone else) or endlessly walking around London (Piper).

In her second year, she moved into a shared flat with two girls who never spoke to her, but left her passive aggressive Post-it notes about every single thing she did. Her music and TV were too loud. She was taking up too much space in the fridge. She'd left a pan to soak in the sink and they would 'appreciate it' if she did her dishes before returning to her room. They'd got the electricity bill – Piper's rent had been inclusive of utilities – and it was much higher than they'd expected, so could she not charge her phone so much or make fewer cups of tea or just, you know, maybe disappear entirely but carry on paying rent. They hadn't written that. But Piper had felt it just the same.

In her third year, she'd moved into a shared house with some other uni friends, ones she actually liked, and Matt, who she'd seen around, but didn't really know. They weren't super close – it wasn't the *Friends* hanging out in each other's rooms, in and out of each other's lives, co-dependent friendship she'd dreamed about, but it had been fine. Gradually everyone had moved out and been replaced until she and Matt were the only ones who'd been there from the start. And they were best friends.

Once she'd finished uni, she'd started temping with a company that specialised in the entertainment industry. She hadn't really known what she wanted to do; all she'd known was that she'd wanted to be in London. And if she was going to temp, she thought she might as well temp in an interesting industry. And she was really good at it. From the very first day she was in demand, moving from one job directly into another.

And she'd enjoyed it. She'd started at Infinite Plays record company, in the Accounts department, basically inputting figures on a spreadsheet. She'd been bored out of her mind, but the people were nice and the office was on the Thames in

Hammersmith and she could actually almost just about see the river out of the window.

Then the PA to the Head of Legal & Business Affairs left suddenly and they asked her to cover for her, just until they found someone else, but by the end of the first week, her boss, John, stopped working on the 'Perfect PA, Central London' ad and started asking her to stay. So she'd stayed.

*

And then there was the money. From her parents' house. From their savings. From their insurance policies. So much money. More money than Piper had really ever dreamed of having. She'd planned to ignore it to begin with. But then she'd bought her flat. For a ridiculous amount of money. She still couldn't really think about how much it had cost. But everyone said it was an investment, that renting was 'dead money' (and then they'd wince when they realised they'd just said the 'd' word to someone who'd just lost her parents). Matt had gone on all the viewings with her. And she'd been glad. Because he had great taste and a very low tolerance for bullshit. There'd been times when Piper had known she would have been snowed by the estate agent, but Matt just said no. At one flat, he refused to let Piper even step over the threshold because of the smell of mould emanating from, apparently, everywhere. Piper had almost settled on a studio in a portered building on actual Abbey Road –it was smaller than she'd wanted, but it had a balcony and she felt safe knowing there was security on site – but then Matt had sent her the details of a flat in Stoke Newington belonging to one of his many friends. It wasn't an area Piper knew or had considered, but the flat was the basement of an adorable end-of-terrace Victorian house and actually had its own private patio garden. Tiny, but still. Piper's heart had fluttered as she'd looked at the photos and then when she and Matt had gone to view it, she'd known before they were even through the front door. It was perfect. It felt like her. No, more than that. It felt like the person she wanted to be. But she hadn't wanted to be alone, so she'd asked Matt to stay. And they'd had so much fun together that he just never left.

CHAPTER SIX

Piper was standing in the queue in Starbucks the following morning when her phone rang. A Merseyside number. She answered it.

'Is that Piper?' a man's voice asked and Piper felt her stomach flip over.

'Yes,' Piper said, shuffling forward as the queue moved a little. 'Who's this?'

'My name's Jim. I'm one of Connie's neighbours? She's okay. You don't need to panic.'

'Oh,' Piper said. She stepped out of the queue and sat down at a nearby empty table. 'What happened?'

'She… I brought her to the walk-in centre. She's just in with them now. She told me not to phone you but—'

'I'm glad you did,' Piper said. 'Thank you. So what happened?'

'When I got up this morning, her door was open. I called out to her, but she wasn't there so I went downstairs to see if she was outside with the dog and she was, but she was… confused.'

'God,' Piper said. She reached for a cup on the table, remembered it wasn't hers, and pushed it away.

'She was in her nightdress. And barefoot. And when I approached her, she didn't know me.'

Piper squeezed her eyes shut, tears burning her throat.

'She seemed to think she was at the house she grew up in. She… she was asking for her mum and her sisters. She said the house had changed and she didn't know who'd done it. She was quite distressed.'

'Okay,' Piper said, her voice tight. 'Okay.'

'I knocked on one of the other neighbours – do you know Beryl? She took her up to the flat and helped her get dressed and then in the car, coming here, she seemed like her normal self again. But… I don't know. I don't know if she had a stroke or… we'll find out, I suppose.'

'Thank you,' Piper said. 'Thank you for finding her and taking her to hospital.'

'It's not the hospital,' Jim said. 'Just the walk-in centre.'

'Yes, sorry,' Piper said. 'But thank you. I really appreciate it.'

'I didn't want to worry you,' he said, clearing his throat. 'But I thought you should know.'

'Thank you,' Piper said again. 'If there's any news can you call me? Or ask her to call me, if she's up to it? I'll phone her later, but just in case there's something…'

'Of course,' he said. 'I'll let you know.'

Piper stayed sitting for a little while, taking deep breaths and waiting for her legs to stop trembling. Then she headed to the bathroom, splashed cold water on her face and sat on the loo, lid down, until her heart rate returned to normal.

Connie couldn't die. Not yet. Piper wasn't ready. There were so many things they still needed to talk about. Piper had so many questions. She knew Connie had boxes of her parents' stuff that she'd told Piper she and Holly needed to go through, but there'd never been a right time.

She should call Holly.

*

'One of us should go up there,' Holly said.

Before ringing her sister, Piper had bought herself a latte and a cheese toastie and texted work to tell them she was going to be late.

'That's what I thought,' Piper said.

'I can't,' Holly said. 'Not this weekend. James has got a dinner tomorrow night –someone from the New York office, and then on Sunday morning I'm playing tennis—'

'Oh yeah,' Piper said, picking a chunk of melted cheese off the crust of her toastie. 'Wouldn't expect you to miss tennis.'

'It's not just tennis,' Holly said. 'It's a networking thing. It's important.'

'Right,' Piper said.

'Are you doing anything?' Holly asked. 'This weekend?'

She'd actually been planning a *RuPaul's Drag Race* marathon with Matt, pizzas, Haribo, and wine – they'd been looking forward to it all week – but she wasn't going to tell Holly that.

'Not really,' she said instead. 'I could probably go.'

'I can pay half your fare, if—'

'I can pay my fare, Hol, thanks,' Piper said, rolling her eyes. 'I'll go up in the morning.'

The faint feeling washed over Piper again – what if that was too late? What if Connie died in the walk-in centre? What if she was dead now?

'She'll be okay,' Holly said. 'She's hard as nails.'

Piper laughed. 'She's old. I keep forgetting how old she is.'

'I know. But this… if this is the first time something like this has happened… Did he say?'

'No.'

'And she was okay last time you saw her?'

Piper tried to remember when that had been. February? For Connie's birthday? She wasn't sure she'd even made it up then. So it would've been Christmas. Nine months ago. Guilt curled her stomach. Although Holly hadn't even made it then: she and James had spent Christmas in Morocco.

'She was a bit forgetful. And she's always repeating stories on the phone. But I wasn't worried, no.'

'Okay,' Holly said briskly. 'So try not to worry too much now. I bet you'll get up there and she'll be her usual self.'

Piper nodded. 'You're right.'

'Let me know, okay? Ring me when you get there.'

'Yeah,' Piper said. 'I will.'

'Cheers,' Holly said. And ended the call.

Piper finished her latte and toastie and wondered how her sister always seemed to weasel out of any family obligations. Not that they had many any more. But Piper was always the one who phoned Connie and then passed any info on to Holly. Piper certainly didn't visit enough, but she visited a lot more than Holly. Neither of them ever wanted to go back to New Brighton, but somehow Holly had mostly managed that, whereas Piper was now booking a return train ticket on her phone.

It was only one night. She was a big girl. She could cope with just one night.

CHAPTER SEVEN

It was always bittersweet for Piper to be back in New Brighton. The memories started to overwhelm her before she even got there. The view of the river from the train. The train announcements, in fact. Even the fabric of the seats. And the distinctive soft plastic smell. Like doll heads. Piper still had no idea what it was.

The station hadn't changed at all – well, they were repairing the loos and so there were a couple of portable toilets outside – but other than that, it was the same as it had always been. Piper could picture herself there as a toddler, holding her parents' hands. She'd left a Beanie Baby on the train once and her dad had brought her back to the station to ask if anyone had handed it in. They hadn't. She'd cried all the way home, up on her dad's shoulders, wiping her snotty fingers in his hair.

But she had to stop thinking about that. Since her parents had died, she'd found the only way to get through these visits was to aggressively push them out of her minds. La la la, everything was fine. They were away on holiday – no, that didn't work – they were just… not here right now. Not gone forever.

She walked along Wellington Road, glancing out over the tops of the houses at the river. It looked calm today. And blue. It didn't always look blue. When she turned up Albion Street, she realised that the enormous hotel that had stood on the corner for her entire life was gone, replaced by a square block of 'luxury flats'. She'd only gone to that hotel once, for someone's wedding reception. The daughter of one of her parents' friends, maybe.

She didn't remember much about it. But still. It was a place that held memories of her parents —her dad standing outside with a cigarette, her mum turning to smile at her as she piled her plate with ham at the buffet — and now it was gone. She knew this was going to happen more and more as time passed. But she hated it.

*

'Connie?' Piper called, barging the sticky front door with her shoulder. Her aunt had buzzed her in downstairs, so couldn't she have opened the actual door to the flat? 'Are you home?'

'Of course I'm home,' she heard from the kitchen. 'Where else would I be?'

'Out?' Piper mumbled, under her breath. She knew better than to actually argue about it. Her aunt's dog, Buster, came skidding down the hall, wriggling with excitement.

'Take him on the balcony!' Connie shouted. 'Before he pees!'

Piper dropped her bag just behind the door and picked Buster up, jogging through the living room to the tiny balcony. As soon as his paws touched tile, Buster let go, looking up at Piper with a distinctly shame-faced expression as a puddle spread under him.

'You are ridiculous,' Piper said, scratching him between his ears. Now that the imminent pee danger had passed, Piper returned to the door and picked up her bag. The narrow hallway had been redecorated since Piper had last been home – there was a huge mirror on one side, reflecting the framed photos of family on the other. Piper glanced at the reflection of the pictures, but didn't linger, heading for the kitchen instead. Her aunt was standing at the sink, elbows deep in soapy water, despite the fact there was a small dishwasher right next to her.

'Did you make it?' she asked.

'Just about. He needs a nappy.'

'Sorry I can't hug you,' Connie said, nodding at the sink.

'I can hug you though.' Piper walked up behind her aunt and looped her arms around her waist, resting her chin on her aunt's shoulder. She felt even thinner than last time she'd seen her, but she smelled the same as she always had: 4711 Cologne and talc.

'I'm fine,' Connie said. 'Don't fuss.'

'I'm not fussing,' Piper said. 'I'm hugging you.'

'There's individual trifles in the fridge,' Connie said.

'I'm okay,' Piper said, crossing the kitchen to flick on the kettle. 'I had something on the train.'

'Later then?' Connie shook her hands – a cloud of dish foam flying up in the air and then settling on the taps – and peeled off her bright yellow washing-up gloves. 'They're low fat.'

If they were the same low-fat trifles Connie had given Piper last time she was home, they were basically a chemical weapon: Piper had taken a mouthful then spat it out into a tissue. Buster had licked the pot clean.

'Train okay?'

'Fine, yeah.' Piper took two mugs down from the cupboard. 'You having tea?'

'I will,' Connie said. 'Thanks. Where's your bag?'

'There.' Piper gestured over her shoulder to her bag on one of the dining chairs.

'So you're not staying long then?'

'Just tonight,' Piper said. 'I've got to be back at work Monday morning.' She was sure she'd told her that on the phone on Friday evening when she'd finally responded to one of Piper's messages.

'Only a bit of a milk for me,' Connie said, as Piper opened the fridge. 'Do you like this colour on the walls? I'm not sure about it.'

Piper hadn't even noticed it was different. It was pale blue now. She had no idea what colour it had been before.

'It's nice,' she said. 'And the hall looks good.'

'I could do without seeing my face every time I come in or go out,' Connie said, on her way out of the kitchen.

As Piper finished making the tea, she listened to her aunt take her bag through to the second bedroom, make her way to the lounge, turn the TV on and off again and then draw a curtain. Piper smiled to herself. She might move house, she might lose weight, but Connie never really changed.

'How long are you staying?' Connie asked, as Piper put the mugs of tea down on the coffee table, before immediately crossing the room to look at the view.

'Just tonight,' Piper said. 'Like I said.'

Between visits, Piper always forgot how her aunt never really listened. Whenever they talked on the phone, Connie told her the same stories, but Piper figured it was because she couldn't remember if she'd told her the last time. Or if it was Piper she'd told or one of her friends. But in person, it was because Connie was constantly distracted. By the dog, or some random bit of housework she'd missed.

Right on cue, Connie tutted and crossed the room to pick something up that Piper couldn't even see. And then she disappeared in the kitchen to, Piper assumed, throw it away. And wipe up whatever tea-making trail Piper had left behind, invisible to any eye other than her aunt's.

After her uncle Graeme had died, Piper had accompanied Connie on the house hunt. Or, rather, flat hunt. Connie had put their house – the house they'd lived in for the whole of their twenty-five years of marriage – on the market only a couple of weeks after Uncle Graeme's funeral. She'd said she couldn't stand to be there without him. Piper had worried at the time that it was too hasty, that she'd regret it, but she never had seemed to. She'd seemed comfortable here right from the start.

Once she'd actually bought the place anyway. The first time they'd come to look, Piper had loved it instantly. It was cosy, but roomy, on a lovely street and high enough for river views. Piper immediately pictured herself on the balcony with a coffee in the morning, a glass of wine in the evening. But Connie hadn't been sure. She'd worried about it being an upstairs flat – even though she'd already rejected all the downstairs flats they'd seen. She'd said the balcony was wasteful. And she didn't like the street because years ago an old boyfriend had lived there and she thought it had given him 'airs'.

'Look at that view!' Piper had said, over and over.

'I don't need a view,' Connie had argued.

Piper had been genuinely worried that Connie wouldn't actually buy it. That she'd go for the tiny place over the shop on the main road, which had a terrace, but the whole flat smelled like meat. Or the one bedroom in the mansion block, where Piper would have to sleep on a sofa bed ('They do very good ones now, apparently.') But then Connie had phoned her and told her she'd already put an offer in and it had been accepted, and she expected Piper to come up and help her pack and then move and then unpack 'since you love the place so much'. And Piper had. And she did love the place. So much. So much, in fact, that she'd actually vaguely thought about buying it if Connie hadn't. For an investment. God knows, everyone had told her she should put her parents' money into property.

And then she'd laughed at herself. As if she'd move back home. As if she'd leave London. As if she'd spend the money her parents had left her on returning to the town she couldn't wait to get away from. As if.

'There was a seal in there the other day,' Connie said from the sofa.

'Where?' Piper turned, but didn't move from the window.

'Marine Lake. Got separated from its family, apparently. Confused. Washed up here.'

'What happened to it?'

Piper braced herself to learn that it had died in some horrible way, but no.

'RSPB came for it,' Connie said. 'No. Not RSPB. The other one.'

'RSPCA?'

'That's it. They gave it a stupid name and took it away to recover. It was on the local news.'

Piper pictured it, all big-eyed and sad. She'd have to google it later. She sat down next to her aunt.

'So. How are you feeling?'

'I saw you on that show, you know?'

Piper bit her lip. She hadn't even considered that Connie would have watched it. She'd never expressed any interest in Piper's blog; in fact Piper had often wondered if Connie had forgotten about it entirely, even though she'd told her about it more than once.

'You did very well, I thought.'

Piper smiled, picking up her tea. 'Thank you.'

'That other woman was a right bitch.'

Piper was glad she hadn't drunk any of her tea. Connie would not have taken kindly to a spit take. 'I don't think I've ever heard you use that word before!'

'I usually say "female dog", ' Connie said. 'But I didn't think it was strong enough this time. Who does she think she is?! I said to Gra—' She stopped. Stared at her tea. Picked the teaspoon out of the sugar bowl and stirred it again. 'I thought the presenter woman should have told her off.'

Piper didn't miss the cut-off mention of Graeme, but she got it. She did the same thing all the time: picked up the phone to call her mum, got excited when she saw Foo Fighters, her dad's favourite band, were touring and started to wonder if they could actually go and see them together or if it would be a bit weird because she and her dad didn't usually do much just the two of them, before remembering. Connie didn't really talk about them. She wasn't actually Piper's aunt, she was her mum's aunt, but she'd always been Aunty Connie because Great Aunty Connie was too much. Piper's mum had always been closer to Connie than to her own mum, who'd moved to Mallorca in the eighties and never came home. The funeral had been the first time the rest of the family – tiny as it was – had seen her for years.

Piper would be lying if she said she wasn't relieved that Connie didn't want to talk about them. Any of them. Piper could talk about it, and she had. To Matt, to friends, even to the bereavement counsellor everyone had told her she should see (she'd gone once, cried solidly for forty-five minutes, and had never gone back), but she didn't need to be talking about them all the time. Particularly not here, when the memories were already overwhelming. (Another plus for Connie's new flat was that there were no memories of her parents there; she didn't have to worry about being ambushed. Apart from the photos, and she could avoid them.)

'Anyway,' Connie said now. 'I thought you did very well. Jenny thought so too. You know, in the pub?'

Piper nodded, even though she wasn't quite sure which one of Connie's friends Jenny was. 'She's been doing Slimming World. She's lost two and a half stone.'

'Oh,' Piper said. That was plenty.

'Have you ever tried that one?' Connie said.

'No,' Piper said. 'I don't diet.'

'Oh no, I know,' her aunt said. 'I was just thinking maybe you could try it.'

That was another thing about her aunt that Piper always forgot.

CHAPTER EIGHT

'I found some things for you,' Connie said later that afternoon.

Connie had been for a nap and Piper had drafted a blog post about travelling by train while fat (in some of the loos she barely had room to pull her knickers up) and replied to some comments and emails on her phone, before watching an episode of *Murder She Wrote* that she'd seen at least twice before. Connie had woken up full of determination, insisting on making a pot of tea and setting out the trifles from hell on the coffee table, before fetching a cardboard box from her bedroom and telling Piper to put her phone away.

'I don't know if you'll be interested,' Connie said. Her cheek was striped with pillow creases. It made Piper's heart hurt. 'And if you're not, then say so and I can give them to someone else. Don't take them home with you and stick them in a charity bag or something.'

'I wouldn't!' Piper said, scratching behind Buster's ears, as he lay panting next to her on the sofa.

'It's not much. Just some bits and bobs I found when I moved. I had boxes and boxes in the loft. Graeme never threw anything out. Even when he told me he'd got rid of stuff, he'd just put it in the loft! He knew I'd never go up that ladder.'

Piper smiled, remembering the time her uncle had put his foot through the ceiling. Connie had been at the bottom of the ladder shouting 'Be careful up there! Stay on the beams!' and then there'd been a crash and his leg had appeared above them all. Piper and Holly had just about managed to keep it together until his slipper had fallen off.

'I don't know if this is your style?' Aunt Connie said, holding out a ring in a navy-blue box. It was a gold band with a flower of diamonds. Piper took it from her and stared at it.

'Is this yours?'

'Yours now,' Connie said. 'If you want it?'

'I can't take this.' Piper was still staring at it. It was so pretty.

'You're not taking it. I'm giving it to you. I got it for fifty years' service. I've never worn it. Never been into rings. Try it on.'

Piper lifted it out of the box and slid it onto the ring finger on her right hand. It looked perfect.

'Gorgeous,' Connie said. 'See, you've always had lovely hands. Not like mine.'

'There's nothing wrong with your hands,' Piper said.

Connie held out her right hand, little finger extended. The tip was missing. Piper had been there when she'd cut it off, chopping potatoes for a shepherd's pie. She'd been totally calm about it too, calling out to Uncle Graeme that she needed him to drive her to the hospital. She'd told Piper and Holly to throw out any potatoes with blood on them, wash the rest and then set them to boil for when she got back. Piper smiled, remembering. Aunt Connie had been kind of a badass.

'Do you want that lamp you used to like?' Connie said now.

'Which…' Piper couldn't think of a lamp she ever would have coveted.

'The spidery one,' Connie said, waving her hands. 'You know. Tiny lights, all…' She wafted her hands again.

Piper frowned. 'I can't think of—'

She was interrupted by a loud bang from the kitchen.

'Oh bloody hell,' Connie said. 'I forgot the blasted pie.'

Piper followed her aunt into the kitchen. 'When did you even put a pie on? Who for?'

'For us,' Connie said. 'For tea.'

'Wait! Don't—' Piper said, but Connie was already lifting a saucepan off the stove and filling it with water from the tap.

'It's fine,' Connie said. 'I've done it before. My memory. You know. And I got chatting. I should've set a timer. I always forget.' She grabbed a strainer, drained the pan, tipped the tin of steak pie into the bin, squirted the pan with washing-up liquid and filled it with hot water, leaving it in the sink to soak. She did it all so fast, Piper hadn't even quite taken in what had happened.

'Was the pie meant to be in the pan?'

'Hmm?' Connie said, her head in the fridge. 'Yes. That's how you cook them. Have you had something to eat?'

'I'm fine, thanks. And there's the trifles.'

'Oh, of course,' Connie said. 'I forgot about them.'

'What did the doctor actually say?' Piper asked, once they were ensconced back in the lounge.

'I told you,' Connie said without looking up.

'You didn't.' Piper had asked – more than once – but her aunt hadn't replied.

'He said I was probably dehydrated. That's all.'

'Hmm,' Piper said.

'Don't "hmm" me. It wasn't as bad as Jim said. He's always been a fusspot. I had a vivid dream and I woke up a bit confused, that's all. You really didn't need to come dashing all the way up here. I'm not dead yet!'

Piper swallowed around the lump in her throat and drank some tea.

'I know,' she said, eventually. 'I just wanted to see you.'

Connie raised one eyebrow at her before delving back into the box.

'I know I don't come home enough,' Piper said. 'It's just hard.'

'I know,' Connie said. 'It's hard for me too. But it's good to see you. I don't see you enough. And as for your sister… I'm not sure I'd recognise her in the street!'

Piper laughed. 'She looks the same. She always looks the same.'

'Skinny and irritable?' Connie said and then giggled. 'Oh, I shouldn't say that. Her heart's in the right place.'

But I'm not sure what it's made of, Piper thought, but didn't say.

CHAPTER NINE

Piper was woken by Buster jumping on her bed and licking her face. She'd carried him out to the balcony, still ninety percent asleep, but when he was still wiggling and yipping half an hour later, she got dressed and took him out for a walk.

From her aunt's house it was only about five minutes' walk to the beach and within a couple of minutes of being outside, Piper was glad she'd forced herself to get up. The sky was blue and dotted with wispy clouds and the air was actually warm. She could smell the salt of the sea and hear the seagulls she could see hovering over marine lake.

The town had changed a lot in the years since Piper had left. None of the cafes and shops on the prom had been there when she'd lived there – the entire development was only a few years old and had transformed the area. When she was younger, there'd been a small boating lake for toy boats and then Marine Lake, which no one really used. Now, Marine Lake was surrounded by restaurants with terraces looking out over the water. It would've been great when Piper and her friends were teens, but instead they'd spent most of their time sitting on a small wall in the park and occasionally pooling their money for chips.

She spent about twenty minutes throwing an increasingly drool-covered tennis ball for Buster, while looking at the worm casts and stepping on the piles of razor clam shells just to hear them crunch.

'Come on then,' she said eventually, when Buster was panting more than he was running and Piper was starting to feel the chill of the morning wind. They walked back up to the prom and Piper headed for Starbucks. Her aunt's bottomless pots of tea were great, but Piper had developed a morning latte habit that jump-started her energy levels even better than the wind off the Irish sea could manage.

*

As she pushed open the door of the coffee shop, latte in one hand, Buster's lead wrapped around her wrist and Buster in exactly the wrong place and doing his best to trip her, Piper looked up and saw Rob.

'No,' she whispered. She wasn't wearing make-up. She couldn't imagine what the wind might have done to her hair. And she hadn't seen Rob for ten fucking years. Just… no.

She took a step back, intending to go back inside the coffee shop, but instead she stood on one of Buster's paws. He yelped. Piper said, 'Oh no! I'm sorry!' and, as she leaned down to comfort him, dropped her latte. When she stood up, Rob was staring straight at her.

'I thought it was you!' he said, walking towards her.

Piper pasted a smile on her face while her brain repeated, *No. No no no no. No.*

He looked both completely different and exactly the same. His body had transformed. He was wearing a black T-shirt and she could see how big his arms had got. He was really broad-shouldered now too and it suited him. He'd been pretty skinny as a teen, but he'd bulked up as well as shot up. But his face, his smile, the way he looked at her like he couldn't believe he'd had the good fortune to bump into her, that was all the same.

'I didn't know you were home!' he said, when he reached her.

'No,' she said. 'I wasn't meant to be. Connie wasn't well and—'

'Are you busy now?' he interrupted. 'Want to get a coffee? I mean, you need to replace that one anyway.'

Piper looked down at the puddle of latte Buster was slurping vigorously. Buster on caffeine. Great.

'Um,' she said. 'Yeah. That would be good. Thanks.'

*

'So is Aunty Connie okay?' Rob asked once they'd torn Buster away from the latte, and were sitting down inside with a new latte for Piper and a black coffee for Rob. 'It's not serious, I hope.'

'She insists she's fine,' Piper said, smiling. She told him what had happened on Friday. 'I think I probably did overreact. I was just scared of something happening to her and me not being here.'

'That's understandable,' Rob said. He leaned back in his chair. 'So. How've you been?'

'I'm good,' Piper said. 'Things are good.'

'Pipes,' Rob said and Piper's face flushed at the old nickname, used so casually. Fifteen years ago, ten years ago, that would have been food for fantasies for days.

'I think you can do better than "good",' Rob said.

'I'm sorry,' Piper said. 'Um. I went to uni. And now I work in a record company. But in the most boring department. I share a flat with my best friend Matt. And I run a body positivity blog. I think that's pretty much it. How about you?'

'You were great on that show,' he said, ignoring her question. 'I couldn't believe it was you. I was getting my breakfast and I heard your voice. You were amazing. You wiped the floor with that woman.'

Piper shook her head. 'I don't remember much about it. But I'm glad you messaged.'

Rob leaned forward, his elbows resting on his knees. 'You never think of messaging me? Or any of the girls?'

Piper's shoulders felt tight, the skin prickling. She'd forgotten how straightforward he was. How when they were teens and the others would lie and bullshit, that Rob would always just come out with things.

'I just... I kind of wanted to leave it all behind, you know?'

'I always worried that maybe we did something? To hurt you?'

She'd forgotten the eye contact thing too. Jesus. She opened her mouth, but no sound came out. She shook her head instead.

'Because if I did, then—'

'You didn't,' Piper said. 'It was me. I just wanted to be away. I wanted to be different. I wanted to start over.'

'And did you?' Rob asked.

Piper smiled. 'I did, yeah. Eventually.'

'Mum sees Connie quite often. In the bank.'

'Yeah, she mentioned that. A few times actually.'

'It's the centre of Mum's social life. Although any time I go anywhere with her she bumps into someone she knows. Drives me nuts.'

Piper laughed. 'I remember that with my parents.' She bit her lip. She didn't want to talk about her parents.

Rob smiled at her, still leaning forward, still staring right at her. 'It's nice though, right? Knowing everyone. Don't get that in London, do you?'

Piper laughed. 'No. But where I live is kind of village-y. So I do know people in shops and the postman – well, we have a postwoman, actually – and everything.'

'Where do you live?'

'Stoke Newington. I love it.' Piper sipped her coffee. 'What do you do?'

Rob grinned. 'I'm a teacher. At Rocklands.'

'No way.'

'You didn't know?'

'No! Connie definitely never told me that. I would've remembered. What's it like?'

'It's great actually. I love it.'

'What do you teach?'

'Design and Technology.'

'Oh my god. Like Mr Rich?'

His face broke into a grin and Piper grinned back at him.

'No! Not like Mr Rich.'

'I bet you're just like him. I bet all the girls are madly in love with you. And some of the boys.'

Rob dropped his head, shaking it as he laughed. 'Nah.'

They would be, Piper knew. They had to be. He was incredibly hot. He'd been gorgeous when they were teens, but now he was… he'd definitely be the teacher everyone fancied.

'What was the name of that teacher…' Rob started to say, looking up at her, his face screwed up in concentration. 'Not Mr Rich. The one with the tight trousers?'

'Mr McGrath,' Piper said, without hesitation. 'God, he was gorgeous.'

'I saw him in a club once. In Liverpool. His wife looks about half his age.'

'Oh god. He was proper gorgeous though. Like… Mr Rich was teacher gorgeous – best of a bad lot, you know? But Mr McGrath was actually gorgeous.'

Rob was actually gorgeous too, she knew. She doubted that any of the other teachers looked anything like him.

'I can't believe you're a teacher,' Piper said, reaching for her latte again. 'You hated school.'

'I didn't hate it,' Rob said. 'I just would have preferred not to be there.'

Rob had been the typical teen who was always getting told off for messing around and joking and distracting the class. It was one of the things Piper had first liked about him – he made everyone laugh, including, often, the teacher. And he and Piper had the same sense of humour. After not very long, they'd look at each other when someone said something stupid or inappropriate or something that could be a double entendre. Piper had loved that she had someone she could glance at, see smiling back at her – or doing a 'look to camera' expression – and be reassured that she wasn't alone, that someone at school got her.

'How's Holly doing?' Rob asked.

'Same as always. Working and working out and going on fancy holidays.'

'She doesn't come home either?' Rob asked.

Piper shook her head and then said, 'Hey! I come home! I'm here now!'

'You are.' He smiled. 'But when are you leaving?'

'Oh shit!' Piper said, glancing at the time on her phone. 'I need to go. Connie'll be wondering where I am and I need to spend a bit more time with her before my train.'

She stood up, bumping the table with her knees, and tried to detangle Buster's lead from the table legs.

'So are you coming to the reunion?' Rob asked, following her out onto the prom.

'What reunion?'

'School reunion. You haven't seen it on Facebook?'

Piper shook her head. She tried to avoid everyone from home on Facebook. And everywhere.

'Weekend after next,' Rob said. 'At the Floral.' He pointed over his shoulder in the direction of the Floral Pavilion Theatre.

Piper's mouth was dry. She really didn't want to go. She'd managed to avoid everyone she used to be friends with for the past ten years – why would she voluntarily walk into a room full of them?

'You should definitely come,' Rob said. 'You know, if you can. I know everyone would be excited to see you.'

Piper shook her head. 'I don't think I can. But I'll have a look. Thanks for telling me.'

She tugged Buster away from the bin he was sniffing and said, 'So I'd better go. It's been really good seeing you.'

'You too,' Rob said.

He took a step closer and pulled her into a hug. He squeezed and she remembered he'd always been great at hugs too.

'Don't leave it so long next time, right?' he said.

She nodded. 'I won't. I promise.'

But she was lying.

CHAPTER TEN

'You should go,' Matt said. It was Saturday morning and he was sitting on the sofa, legs stretched out across Piper's lap and feet up on the side. The fibre-optic lamp – the tiny lights Connie had talked about – was in pride of place on the side table, switched on even though you could barely see it in the light. Matt had been delighted with it, calling it 'a fugly seventies classic' and taking dozens of photos of it for Instagram.

But since then they'd barely seen each other all week. Matt had a project on at work that meant he left early and got back late, and even though they'd texted about the reunion, they hadn't had a chance to properly discuss it until now.

'Fuck off,' Piper said mildly, pushing his legs away.

'You should,' he said. 'Closure. Also…' He sat up, pushing his face close to hers. 'You might enjoy it.'

'I wouldn't enjoy it,' she said, pushing him back down again. 'Does anyone enjoy school reunions? They're always awful on TV.'

'TV isn't real. I can't believe I have to keep telling you.' He gestured at the screen with the remote.

'Some of it is. David Attenborough is.'

'That's just what they want you to believe. I'm not even sure David Attenborough's not animatronic. Anyway I went to mine and it was fucking great.'

'Because you got hammered and punched someone and shagged someone else and then… I can't remember, stole something?'

'Streaked,' Matt corrected. 'You've missed out the most important details. I punched the twat who bullied me for years and I shagged the girl who wouldn't even have looked at me at school.'

'Because you were fat,' Piper said.

'Yeah,' Matt agreed. 'And also the hair and the nose and the glasses and spots. But—'

'I'm still fat,' Piper said. 'In fact, I'm fatter than I was at school. And they called me lard arse back then.'

'So?' Matt shrugged. 'You're gorgeous. And successful. And confident. With norks for days. Wear that gold sequinned skirt and that black crossover top. And your biker boots.'

'Fuck's sake,' Piper said. That was actually a really great suggestion. She could see herself in that exact outfit. Maybe with bright pink lipstick and tassel earrings. 'I'm not going.'

'Robbie wants you to go though. He wouldn't have mentioned it if he didn't want to see you.'

Piper rolled her eyes. 'He was just being polite.'

'Nah. I can picture it now. He'll be at the far side of the room. You'll walk in and the lights'll be low, dry ice swirling, tinsel hanging from the ceiling—'

'Tinsel?'

'Don't they have tinsel at these things? You'll have your twinkle umbrella—'

'That's *Buffy*.'

'Or maybe he'll be on stage with his electric guitar—'

'That's *Back to the Future*.'

'It doesn't matter. It'll be like everyone else in the room has disappeared and—'

'Someone'll drop a bucket of pig's blood on my head.'

'If that happens I'll give you a million quid.'

'You haven't got a million quid.'

'I'll borrow it. That's how confident I am that no one's going to drop a bucket of blood on you.'

'I know. That's not going to happen. But...'

Piper leaned back and rested her head on the back of the sofa. Matt sat up and leaned into her side, his head on her shoulder.

'It could be good for you, you know?'

'I know. I mean, I know that's the theory. But if I'd wanted to keep in touch with any of them, I would've done, you know?'

'I know. But you also have a tiny bit of a tendency – and this isn't a criticism, just an observation and you know I say it with love – to push people away. Particularly when you feel like you've fucked up.'

Piper sighed and turned it into a groan. 'I know. But I moved away. I don't live there any more. I've got new friends. Why do I have to go back?'

'You don't have to,' Matt said. 'But I think it might be a good thing. And where else are you going to wear that skirt?'

'Ugh. I hate it when you're right.'

'Sucks to be you then since I'm always right.' Matt nuzzled into her neck and blew a raspberry behind her ear. 'Want me to come with you?'

'God no,' Piper said, turning to kiss him on the temple. 'The only thing more pathetic than turning up alone would be taking my BFF with me.'

'I could pretend to be your boyfriend. Fondle you inappropriately. Tell them all how hot you are in bed. How I can't keep up with your constant demands for my dick.'

'Please stop talking. I don't want to bring my cornflakes back up.'

'I will though,' Matt said. 'If you want me to.'

'I know you would. That's why I love you.'

'You're going to go.'

Piper opened her eyes and stared up at the ceiling. 'I'm going to think about going, yes.'

'You must be intrigued though. About Rob, Robbie, the Robster.'

'Rob is fine. I am, yeah, a bit. It's just… been a long time.'

'You could sleep with him and break his heart,' Matt suggested. 'Would that help?'

Piper laughed. 'It wouldn't hurt.'

But she didn't want to break his heart. And she absolutely wanted to see him again. She just didn't want to have to go home and face all of her old friends in order to do it.

'Ugh,' she said. 'I hate being a grown-up.'

'Life is hard and so am I,' Matt said, as he always did. 'But you are a badass and you can totally do this.'

'If you say so.'

'Now can you take your bad ass to the kitchen and make me a brew? I'm parched.'

*

'I've thought about it some more,' Matt said that afternoon as they wandered down the high street, poking in and out of shops and picking up random bits that they needed for the flat –light bulbs, bin liners, garlic, tomatoes, eggs and chicken for the shakshuka Matt said he was making for dinner. 'And you definitely have to go.'

'I definitely don't,' Piper said. She was holding a bag of kale and wondering if she should get it and google ways to make it not taste like shit or just accept that she was never going to be a person who ate kale.

'Put that back,' Matt said, taking it out of her hands and dropping it back in the crate. 'I'll do spinach. Kale is evil. But listen, I'll tell you why.'

'I assumed you would.'

'You're not the same person you were at school,' Matt said.

They were in the queue now, Piper standing slightly behind him. 'I know that.'

'No. I mean it. I know you say you know that, but I'm not sure you do. And that's why I think you should go home.'

'To prove to myself that I'm not the same person?'

'Yes,' Matt said. They were at the front now. The guy on the checkout was cute. Skinny with dyed silvery-grey hair and a nose piercing.

'Hey,' Matt said. 'How are you?'

The guy dipped his head and looked up at Matt from under his eyelashes. Seriously?

'You never called,' he said, his voice low.

Piper looked at Matt, one eyebrow raised.

'I know,' Matt said. 'I'm sorry. Something came up.'

Piper rolled her eyes. If there'd been aubergines nearby, she would've grabbed one and chucked it in the basket as a visual reminder of how obvious they were being, but no, they were on the other side of the shop.

'You've still got my number though, right?' the boy said.

'Of course.'

Piper couldn't take any more. 'I'll see you outside.'

In front of the shop, she leaned on the wall and scrolled through her phone. Someone had commented 'fat bitch' on her latest Instagram photo – the preview for her blog post – so she deleted that. The rest of the comments were lovely, from 'slay' to 'that lipstick really suits you' to 'you did so well!' and 'that woman needs a good meal'. She wanted to reply to that one – quite a lot of the comments about the debate had disparaged Naomi's looks or body or personality and it made Piper feel sick. In fact, she should probably write a blog post about it – a comment wouldn't be enough. She made a mental note to do that later and flicked over to Facebook.

Robbie – Rob – had messaged her earlier in the week to say it had been great to see her and he really hoped she'd come to the reunion, but she hadn't replied. She'd meant to –she'd been trying to think of how to say that it wasn't going to happen – but then she'd left it too long and to message now would be weird.

Instead, she tapped the search box and typed in Mel's name. She'd been her best friend at school. She lived on the next road so they'd walked to and from school together every day and sat together in the classes they'd shared. But she hadn't been Mel's best friend, that had been Dawn. Piper had liked Dawn too – she was hilarious. But she'd been loud and disruptive in a way that had made Piper uncomfortable.

Mel looked pretty much the same. Piper had clicked on her profile enough to know that. She'd also tried to add Piper as a friend more than once, but Piper had always deleted the request. She'd thought when she moved to London that it was going to be a clean slate, that she could leave everything behind and start again, but it hadn't quite worked out like that. And occasionally she'd felt a little envious thinking that her friendship group might still be friends. Without her. But they probably didn't miss her at all. Not really.

'What's your damage?' Matt said, coming out of the shop and bumping her with his hip.

'Your flirting was upsetting the fruit,' she said, pushing her phone into the side pocket of her bag.

'You're just jealous.'

'Sure,' Piper said, smiling. 'That's it exactly. Where did you meet him anyway?'

Matt frowned. 'I've been trying to remember. Party, I think. He was very bendy, I remember that much.'

'God,' Piper said. 'I did not need to know that.'

'Lovely hands,' Matt added.

'Shut up now.'

They walked a little further down the high street and Matt said, 'Would it be ridiculous to get a coffee here when we could just go home?'

'Yes,' Piper said, but she was already pushing the door open. The coffee shop was through a florists and out in a courtyard and it was one of her favourite places. She found a table and put their bags down, while Matt went to order. She took her phone out again and opened Facebook. She should write a pros and cons list – that's what she would usually do.

But she knew she should go home. She should go home, go to the reunion, see her friends, check up on Connie and then come back to London and forget all about it. That would be the sensible thing to do. And she always did the sensible thing.

She tapped on Rob's message and typed in *Sorry it's taken me so long to get back to you. Was good to see you too. See you at the reunion!*

Then she put her phone away and smiled up at Matt as he appeared with their lattes and two ridiculously indulgent-looking cakes.

'Couldn't resist,' Matt said.

CHAPTER ELEVEN

Holly was late. Which wasn't like her. At all. Piper had sat outside the cafe – even though it wasn't exactly warm, it was a bright, sunny, day and Piper would always rather be outside if she had the opportunity. Plus Holly's voice tended to carry so Piper always felt better when there was more space for it.

She scrolled through her phone for a little while before making herself put it away, tucking it down inside her bra. Rob had replied yesterday with 'YESSSS!' and said that he was looking forward to seeing her again – 'and the girls will be too.' Every time Piper thought of seeing Mel and Dawn again her stomach fluttered with nerves. And she hadn't even let herself think about whether Claire, her teen nemesis, would be there.

She looked up at the blue sky, the wispy white clouds, the tops of the pastel-painted buildings. She was so lucky to be living here. This was exactly what she'd always wanted, what she'd dreamed of. So the path to it hadn't been what she'd imagined, but that didn't matter, did it? If it got her to the same place?

She watched a group of girls sifting through the jewellery outside a store on the opposite corner. They called to each other, holding up necklaces and brooches, laughing and snapping photos on their phones. Piper thought they were maybe Spanish. On holiday or studying? Or maybe they were just pretending to be Spanish. Piper and her friends had done that once, in Liverpool. Getting the ferry over, pretending to be American tourists, all talking in dreadful accents picked up from *Friends* mostly. She'd told a guy on a market stall on Church Street that she was from Tulsa, Oklahoma, over on a cultural exchange. Mel, of course, said she was from New York – she was a dancer and she'd come over to study at LIPA, the performing arts school. Piper would never have thought of that. Not that anyone would have believed it of her anyway. They believed Melissa.

'Sorry,' Holly said, dropping into the seat opposite Piper.

Piper jumped a little. Lost in her own thoughts, she'd half-forgotten she was even expecting anyone.

'Tube was fucked,' Holly said.

She unwound a blue scarf from her neck and then shrugged her coat off her shoulders, letting it drop down onto the chair behind her.

'It's not warm enough to sit outside,' she said. 'We should go in once we've ordered.'

'It's not that bad,' Piper said. 'It's nice.' And Holly had just taken her scarf and coat off, so she couldn't be that cold.

'You're never cold,' Holly said, shrugging. She yanked the menu out of the wooden box it was tucked into, along with cutlery and napkins. 'Have you been here before?'

Piper shook her head and then realised her sister wasn't looking. 'No. I've heard good things though.'

'From who?' Holly said, and glanced up at Piper. Her face was almost a sneer and Piper actually jerked back in her seat a little.

'Loads of people,' Piper said. 'Matt.'

'Ugh, Matt,' Holly said, as she always did.

Piper smirked to herself. She didn't usually have to mention Matt quite so early in her meetings with Holly. But today she seemed to be in a particularly snotty mood. Holly loved Matt. Holly loved Matt in a way Piper had never seen Holly love anyone, even her husband. Holly turned into an entirely different person around Matt and Piper couldn't get enough of it. Matt said Piper was cruel. That of course Holly went to pieces around him because he was so gorgeous and amazing. And if he flirted with Holly a little, it was because Holly was hot, not because he wanted to make Piper laugh.

'What did he recommend?' Holly said, glancing up again. 'Matt.'

'Oh!' Piper said. 'I can't remember if he did... I think he mentioned the pulled pork thing, but that might have been somewhere else.'

Holly pulled a face. 'What are you having?'

'Duck and sweet potato hash. It comes with kale but I can leave that. And a Bloody Mary.'

'It's eleven a.m.,' Holly said.

'Perfectly acceptable brunch drink.' Piper took out her phone, saw she had no notifications, and put it back.

'You shouldn't do that,' Holly said.

'What?'

'Keep your phone in your bra.'

'I don't keep it there. I've just put it in there for now.'

'James told me he read a thing that said it can cause breast cancer.'

'Hmm,' Piper said. That sounded unlikely. It sounded like the video someone once sent her of someone frying eggs with a phone. She wanted to take her phone back out and google it, but she forced herself to resist.

'I'm going to have the smashed avocado,' Holly said, putting the menu down on the table. 'And a skinny latte.'

Piper's stomach rumbled and she craned her neck to look inside the cafe, to see if a waiter was coming outside.

'That's the other problem with sitting outside,' Holly started to say, but a waitress appeared at the end of the table and smiled at them both.

'Could I have the duck and sweet potato hash?' Piper said. 'And a Bloody Mary. And a glass of tap water.'

'I'll have the same,' Holly said.

Once the waitress had gone, Piper stared at her sister.

'What?' Holly said.

'What happened to smashed avocado and a skinny latte?'

Holly closed her eyes briefly, reaching back behind herself to grab her coat.

'I just… that's what I always have. When we go to brunch.' She meant her and her husband, not her and Piper. She and Piper hadn't been to brunch for months. 'And I just suddenly thought… fuck it.'

'Wow,' Piper said. Although she was already low-key worried that Holly wouldn't like the hash and/or the cocktail and Piper would get the blame.

'So,' Piper said. 'How's things?'

'Oh you know. The usual. I think you've probably got more to tell me than I have you.'

She somehow managed to make that sound like Piper had been indulging in levels of debauchery Holly would barely recognise.

'Aunty Connie says hello,' Piper said.

'How was she?'

Piper frowned. 'Older. And she repeats stuff a lot more. The flat wasn't really clean. I don't know… she was okay. Insisted she was fine and that Jim had totally overreacted. But… I don't know.'

'Shit,' Holly said.

'I know. I think we need to go home more often.'

'I can't,' Holly said, immediately. 'Work is completely insane. And James's is not much better.'

'You could manage once a month, surely?' Piper suggested.

Her sister shook her head. 'Once a quarter maybe?'

Who even measured time in quarters outside of the financial industry?

'I'm going again next weekend,' Piper said. 'I'm going to the school reunion.'

'Wow,' Holly said, her eyebrows somewhere up near her hairline.

'What?'

Before her sister could answer, the waitress reappeared with their drinks: two Bloody Marys and a jug of water with glasses. Piper swirled her drink with the celery stalk.

'You've spent years avoiding home, avoiding your friends, and now you're going back for the second time in a month?' Holly asked.

Piper blinked. 'I know. I just... It's hard, going back. But I have to go back to see Connie and I bumped into Robbie and—'

'Ah,' Holly said.

'What?'

'That's why you're going. Because of Robbie.'

'No. Not just because of him. He messaged me after—'

'After you were on TV.'

'Yes. He saw me on *Hey, UK!* And he messaged me and then I bumped into him when I was home and we had coffee and caught up and it was really great. And then he mentioned the reunion and I thought... why not?'

'You are so naive,' Holly said. 'You've always been naive.'

'What am I being naive about?'

'He only contacted you because he saw you on TV. Obviously.'

'But... why? I'm not famous. I can't do anything for him. Why would you think—'

Holly shook her head. 'I just don't think it's a good idea for you to start rushing up there every month. We can sort someone out to check in on Connie and you should get back on Tinder again.'

Piper pinched her own thigh through the fabric of the stripy dress she was wearing. She didn't think she was dreaming, but Holly was being so weird that maybe it was just a particularly vivid one. But no. Ow.

'What are you talking about?' Piper said, incredulous.

Holly blew out a breath. 'It doesn't matter. Ignore me.'

'No. Tell me. What's the problem with me going home? Seeing Rob? He goes by Rob now, by the way, not Robbie.'

'Of course he does.' She shook her head. 'Nothing. Nothing's wrong with it. You should do what you want.'

'Thanks,' Piper said. 'I will.'

They both took out their phones – Piper from her bra, Holly from her bag – and Piper spent the next ten minutes messaging Matt about Holly being even weirder than usual, while Matt responded with suggestions for things Piper could tell Holly about Matt to increase her weird crush, eventually sending a shirtless, duckface, mirror selfie that made Piper yelp with laughter.

'What?' Holly said. The first word she'd uttered for ten minutes. She'd mostly been focussed on huffing and furiously texting Piper didn't even know who.

'Matt sent me a selfie. Want to see?' She was joking. Holly wasn't keen on selfies either. Piper was surprised when she nodded, looking oddly nervous.

'Seriously?' She turned her phone round to show Holly. Holly's face did something Piper wasn't sure she'd ever seen it do before. She looked sort of slack, like she was about to faint clean away, then scared, and then an expression Piper couldn't quite identify passed over, before she managed to wrestle it into a forced smile.

'Loves himself, that one,' she said.

'Oh he absolutely does,' Piper said. 'It's one of the things I love the most about him.'

Holly shook her head almost imperceptibly.

'Want me to forward it to you?' Piper joked.

When her sister didn't answer, she looked up and saw that odd expression again. What was it?

'Seriously?' Piper said again.

Holly frowned. 'No. Of course I don't. God's sake.'

The food, when it arrived, was unbelievably delicious. Piper had eaten almost a quarter when she thought to ask Holly what she thought.

'It's really good,' Holly said. She had a smear of crème fraiche at the corner of her mouth. 'The Bloody Mary is too. Can't remember the last time I had a drink in the day.'

'God,' Piper said. 'You need to loosen up.'

'Understatement of the year, right there,' Holly said.

Piper had been telling her sister she needed to loosen up for as long as she could remember. She didn't think she'd ever agreed with her before.

'Hol,' she said now, swirling a piece of duck through sriracha sauce. 'Is everything okay?'

'No,' she said, still looking down at her plate. She'd also separated the duck from the sweet potato from the kale, Piper noticed. 'But it will be. Just some work bullshit.'

Piper had assumed Holly would want to go as soon as they'd finished their food, but she actually suggested getting lattes and Piper found that she wasn't quite ready to go either. She and Holly had never been best friends, probably never would be, but she was clearly going through something and Piper wanted to try and help if she could.

CHAPTER TWELVE

Piper spent Monday morning at work trying to come up with a name for the girl band. Another memo had been sent with a list of equally terrible names and a link to an audio file of the girl's demo. Piper had listened to it with headphones and had been surprised by how much she liked it – it was catchy and fresh and they all had great voices that worked well together. She hated to think of them being saddled with a name like 'Sugar or Spice' for their entire career.

She googled 'girl band names' and ended up falling down a girl band YouTube hole. She was interrupted by John tapping her on the shoulder. She pulled her ear buds out and smiled up at him.

'Sorry.'

'Is this work?'

'Sort of.' She grinned. 'I was trying to find a name, but I got a bit carried away.'

'I did the same last night,' John said. 'Although I watched sixties girl group videos not…' He gestured at Piper's computer screen.

'B*witched,' she said.

'What about something like… Curves?' he said. 'Or Figure Eight? Hourglass?'

'God,' Piper said, before she could stop herself. 'I don't know that—'

'No,' John said, pushing his glasses up on his head and immediately putting them back on again. 'Maybe not. Keep trying, eh?'

'Will do.'

*

'So shall we just go to The Chancellors?' Piper said, as she and Lee left the building at the end of the day.

He'd waited for her in reception, sitting on the sofa, flicking through the latest issue of Q on the coffee table. It was the same one Matt had been reading. At the thought of Matt, Piper wondered if he'd ended things with Becks yet or if he was going to let it drag on even longer. He didn't have the best track record with ending relationships, preferring to let his partners get fed up of him rather than take any action himself.

'Nah,' Lee said. 'I thought we could go to The Dove, have you been there?'

Piper shook her head. 'Haven't even heard of it. Where is it?'

'Just along the river. It's about ten minutes' walk.'

'Cool,' Piper said.

It was a nice evening, sunny, but with a cool breeze off the river. Piper had spent the day stuck at her desk, working on the still-unnamed girl band's contract without even a break for lunch, so she was glad to get outside.

'Do you live near here?' Lee asked, as they started to walk.

Piper shook her head. 'Stoke Newington. Bit of a pain of a commute, but I love it there. How about you?'

'Enfield,' he said. 'Used to live in Vauxhall, but I split up with my girlfriend and moved back with my parents for a bit to save some money.'

'That sounds sensible,' Piper said.

'Are your parents in London?' Lee asked.

Piper looked out over the river, and bit the inside of her cheek. At least she was going to get it out of the way.

'No,' she said. 'They're dead.'

'Woah,' Lee said. 'I'm sorry. I didn't know. That's awful. Was it cancer or…?'

Piper was always surprised when someone asked her outright how they'd died. People sometimes hinted around it, asking if they'd been ill or if it had been sudden, whether they'd died close together or how old she'd been when she'd lost them. But it was rare for someone to both ask and guess a cause.

'No,' she said, as they passed under the bridge. 'They were in an accident. On holiday. Dad died instantly and Mum the following week in hospital.'

'Fuck,' Lee said. 'That's brutal!'

'Yeah,' Piper said. 'It was.'

'How old were you?'

They were passing a row of houses that Piper loved and she was annoyed knowing that in future, whenever she walked along this strip of river, she'd remember this conversation. Until now, she'd always tried to work out who lived in such perfect homes in a perfect position, but not any more. Next time she knew she'd hear Lee saying 'That's brutal!' She should probably leave. Make an excuse and go home. But she assumed they were almost there and she didn't want to be rude, since they worked together. Plus now she wanted a drink.

'We could go to the The Blue Anchor?' Piper suggested, seeing the pub's distinctive bright blue picnic benches up ahead. They went there with work quite often, for lunch sometimes, or drinks after.

'Gets too busy,' Lee said. 'The Dove's quieter. You'll like it. There's a terrace overlooking the river.'

They were literally passing The Blue Anchor's terrace overlooking the river and half the benches were empty, not too busy at all. But fine. They passed The Rutland Arms, which she'd also been to with work. And once with Matt for the Sunday roast when he'd insisted on a weekend walk along the river, but lost interest after about twenty minutes.

They passed Furnival Gardens, where she and Matt had stood and watched a man standing on top of one of the canal boats (that were apparently moored but frequently simply looked wedged in the not particularly pleasant-smelling black mud), crafting folding chairs from piles of wood. He sawed and sanded and hammered and varnished, all while wearing cut-off jeans and a loose black vest, his long golden hair tied up in a messy bun. She and Matt had been transfixed and Matt still talked about him sometimes. The one that got away. Slowly. Sitting on a hand-made chair on top of a canal boat.

'It's just here,' Lee said, pointing vaguely.

It was no wonder Piper hadn't been aware of it before. The pub was tucked away like a secret, down a narrow lane behind the gardens. Lee opened the door and Piper followed him inside. It was similar to The Chancellors – the pub she went to with Matt whenever he met her from work. Dark and cosy, not at all a gastro pub. An old man sat at the small table just behind the door, a pint on the table in front of him, a sad-looking dog on the floor at his feet.

Three steps led to a second level just next to the bar and Lee headed up there, Piper following. The pub was a maze of small, interconnected rooms, almost all of them empty. Lee rejected one where a woman sat nervously in the corner, holding her handbag on her knee, and then eventually chose one with a partial view of the river and a fireplace in the opposite corner. The fire wasn't lit. So much for the terrace.

'Drink?' Lee asked.

'Gin and tonic please.'

He headed to the bar, while Piper sat down, sliding a cardboard beer mat towards herself. This place actually reminded her of a pub at home she and her friends had all tumbled into one night. She couldn't remember where they'd been, just that they were giddy and laughing, the boys shouting and shoving each other, the girls outwardly calmer, but clutching each other, bright-eyed and over-excited.

There'd been three men in the pub who, faced with six teenagers clearly too young to drink, had all just stared at them blankly until they turned and left. They'd talked about it for ages, making it more and more dramatic in the retelling until it even included a needle scratching across a record, silencing the music that hadn't, in reality, been playing (song choice had wavered for a while – they'd started with 'something Elvis' and finally settled on Lionel Ritchie's 'Dancing on the Ceiling', which Robbie claimed was suitably creepy in the setting and everyone else just thought was hilarious). Someone added a barman cleaning a pint glass with a tea towel who'd tried to communicate just with his eyes that if they'd stayed they'd be in danger, someone else a dog standing slowly, teeth bared, hackles raised. More often than not, they couldn't get the words out for laughing.

Lee came back with the drinks and sat down opposite Piper, smiling. He suddenly seemed nervous and while Piper hadn't been nervous as they'd walked to the pub, butterflies now started to flutter in her belly. It wasn't Lee. It was just the entire concept of a date. It had been a while.

*

An hour later and Piper wished she'd left it even longer. Lee was sort of... shifty. Whenever anyone came near the room, he flinched and moved his chair incrementally until he had his back to the doorway. Plus they really didn't have anything in common. They talked about work, tried another topic that went nowhere, then went back to talking about work over and over. And he really didn't have anything good to say about his job. His colleagues were useless, he claimed he never got the same opportunities that were handed to literally everyone else and he didn't even know what Piper's job was, asking her how things were in Accounts when she actually worked in Legal.

'I think I need to head back,' Piper said, when he inexplicably suggested getting a third drink.

'Yeah?' Lee said. 'I'll walk you to the Tube.'

Piper had already wondered if there was a way to get out of that, but she hadn't come up with anything. Still, it was only another ten minutes. They left the pub and headed up the lane around the back of the gardens. They'd only taken a couple of steps when Lee slid one hand down Piper's arm and used it to turn her towards him. He stepped up close, pressing her back against the wall, and leaned in for a kiss.

'Um…' Piper said.

'Oh god!' he said, stepping back. 'Sorry. I just thought—'

'It's okay,' Piper said. 'I just… I really need to get back. It takes an hour and that's if I don't miss the bus, so…'

'Yeah,' Lee said. He wasn't meeting her eyes but then again he had spent quite a lot of the last hour looking at her cleavage. 'Sorry. Let's go.'

The walk to the Tube took place mostly in silence. Piper asked him a couple of questions about how long he planned to stay home with his parents, where he thought he'd live when he'd saved up enough, but she mainly got just one word answers. By the time they hit King Street, she'd given up altogether. It was only when they got to the station that Piper realised they were both getting the same line. And it was only when they were seated on the Tube that they realised they were both going to Finsbury Park. They tried to make awkward conversation as far as Earl's Court, but then gave up and took out their phones. Piper read a book while Lee played some game with red and blue dots that made him mutter 'fuxache' under his breath every few minutes.

They got off the Tube at Finsbury Park, walked to the bus stop, and were finally able to go their separate ways. Piper couldn't even read on the bus, she just rested her head on the window and stared out at the world.

*

'How did it go?' Matt called from the sofa, as soon as Piper was through the front door.

'Awful,' she said, kicking off her shoes and shrugging off her coat. 'I somehow managed to arrange the world's most drawn-out bad date.'

She told him about it as she poured herself a glass of wine and sat on the sofa next to him, pulling her feet up underneath her.

'What are we watching?'

'Documentary about Tom Petty,' he said.

Piper stood up again and fetched her laptop from her bag. She might as well get another blog post drafted and ready.

Matt nudged her thigh with his foot. 'You look delish, by the way. No wonder Boring Colleague tried to snog you in a hedge.'

Piper snorted. 'That was weird. There was no way he could've thought I was up for it.'

'Probably thought he might as well get a quick fumble out of it,' Matt said, without looking up. 'You know, so the evening wasn't a total write-off.'

'Lovely. How romantic.'

'Men are pigs.'

'Sing it, sister.'

Piper had almost finished the blog post – about the shoes she'd been wearing that day along with some musings on walking while fat – when Matt uncurled himself from the sofa and then stopped, saying 'Pass us your phone.'

'Why?'

'Just give it here.'

'You're not thinking of messaging Rob, are you? Or Lee?' But she was already handing it over.

'Course not. What do you take me for?' He snapped a photo and handed the phone back to her. 'Look how great you look.'

Piper was rolling her eyes before the phone was even back in her hand, but she stopped when she saw it.

'Wow.'

'Right? I quite fancy pushing you into a hedge myself.'

'Shut up,' she muttered, turning up the brightness so she could see the photo better. She was leaning back on the sofa, her laptop balanced on one thigh, her other leg bent at the knee, foot on the edge of the cushion. She was staring into the phone – at Matt – with a 'what now?' expression. She looked tired, but determined. She looked big and soft and comfortable. She looked in the photo exactly how she looked in her own head and always struggled to capture in photos.

'You should take all my photos,' she said, immediately clicking through to Instagram.

'No way,' Matt said, heading for the bathroom. 'I'm no one's Instagram bitch.'

Piper uploaded the photo, added a couple of filters just to even out the colour and captioned it 'My happy place is on the sofa with bae (my laptop)'.

CHAPTER THIRTEEN

Making herself walk in was the hardest part. As she'd known it would be. But Piper had gone to the loo and done the Wonder Woman Power Pose first, staring herself down in the mirror. She knew she was meant to say affirmations aloud, but she certainly wasn't going to risk someone walking in and overhearing her mumbling 'You are a badass bitch' at her reflection, so she just thought them instead: *You are awesome. You can do this. You're not the girl you used to be. You are strong with amazing tits.*

Her tits did actually look amazing: the sequinned silver kimono dress she was wearing had a plunging neck and a twisted waist that made her boobs look even better than usual. She loved it. And her silver shoes. And her bright pink lipstick. She grinned at herself in the mirror. She looked good. She felt... terrified, but that was fine – she just needed to get out there, get a drink and find someone to talk to.

She pushed open the door and stood there for a second, looking around the room. It was square and plain – cream walls and ceiling, polished wood floor – but with, at one end, floor to ceiling windows overlooking the river and the fort. The ceiling was dotted with small lights flashing different colours – pink, blue, orange, green – and a long table ran along the far side, the buffet already set out but covered with cling film and foil. Chairs and small tables were dotted around the edges of the room, leaving a space at the centre for the dancefloor, but as yet no one was dancing.

There was no one she recognised. No one to talk to. And though it was possible there were people there she'd known at school, she didn't want to risk getting saddled with a virtual stranger for the evening. So she made a beeline for the bar instead. She was on her second gin and tonic when Rob walked in. She would have seen and recognised him instantly even if the room had been heaving, but attendance was still pretty sparse. A few people had arrived since Piper, including one of her PE teachers with a much younger man hanging off her, but still no one she wanted to talk to. Rob was the first of her friend group to arrive.

He was wearing a navy suit and a white shirt and he looked… Piper drained her drink. She didn't know whether she should approach him or wait for him to find her. She didn't know how to stand. How did she usually stand? Where did she keep her arms? She put one hand on her hip – half Power Pose? – and gripped her empty glass with the other.

'Another, love?' the barman asked.

Piper made a sound, but she couldn't have said what it was. Or what it was meant to be. She felt like Rob was moving in slow motion. Like when the female love interest was introduced in a film with a wind machine. There was no wind machine. And no slow motion. But if Rob was moving at normal speed, why was he still over by the door? He was looking around, but didn't appear to have seen Piper yet. Unless he'd seen her and was pretending not to see her. Piper wished her brain would shut the fuck up.

'That's four,' the barman said, pushing another drink towards Piper's hand.

'Three. That's my third,' she said, tearing her eyes away from Rob. The barman had tramlines shaved into his left eyebrow. Was that still a thing?

'Four quid,' the barman said. And grinned.

'Oh god,' Piper said, shaking her head at herself. 'Sorry.'

'Old boyfriend?' He nodded towards Rob.

'No.' She took a fiver out of her bag and passed it over, before picking up the glass and taking a sip. 'Just a friend.'

The barman handed over her change and she dropped it, loose, into her tiny bag.

Rob hadn't made it much further into the room. The guy who'd arrived with Miss Crowley, the PE teacher, was talking to him, laughing and gesturing. Rob looked slightly confused. Piper wondered if Miss Crowley's boyfriend had been at school with them, but she didn't recognise him. Also that would be gross. Although Miss Crowley was hot. Half the school had had a crush on her.

Why was she glued to the bar pondering her old PE teacher's love life? It was getting ridiculous. She'd been hiding for long enough. If Rob wasn't going to come over, she'd have to go over to him. She pulled her shoulders back, pushed her chest out and… nothing. She couldn't do it. Fuck. Maybe one more drink. Even though she'd promised herself she wouldn't get drunk.

'Piper?'

She knew that voice. She turned to see Maxine Williamson smiling at her. Oh god.

'How are you?' Maxine said.

Maxine looked exactly the same as she had at school. Exactly. Piper suspected she'd even had that same dress back then: a tight red vest dress with a lacy shrug over the top.

'You look amazing,' Maxine said. 'I love your dress.'

Piper smiled. Maxine had been kind of annoying at school. Clingy and needy. But she had no side to her and she'd always been sweet to Piper. Every now and then Piper had tried to casually withdraw from the friendship, but Maxine had never taken the hint.

'You too,' Piper said. 'It's good to see you.'

Maxine smiled at her. 'Still living in London?'

Piper had just started to reply when Maxine put her hand on her forearm and squeezed. 'Have you seen Robbie?'

'Um,' Piper said.

'He looks so hot. You had such a crush on him, remember?'

Piper shook her head. 'I didn't. We were friends and—'

'You told me you did,' Maxine said. 'Don't you remember?'

God. 'Oh yeah.' Piper forced out a laugh. 'I'd forgotten that.'

She'd told Maxine she had a crush on Rob and Maxine had told her she'd once given a teaching assistant a handjob in the school car park. It hadn't really seemed like a fair exchange of information.

'He's coming over,' Maxine said, her voice squeaking a little with excitement. Just the sound of it took Piper all the way back to school. The two of them standing on the upstairs balcony, looking down at Robbie in the hall downstairs. Maxine asking Piper why she didn't just ask him out. Why? Why? Why?

But she was right. Robbie *was* coming over. He was walking across the dancefloor towards them. In slow motion. With his suit jacket blown back by a wind machine, hair ruffling lightly. Piper blinked. Yeah, he was just walking towards them normally, like a person.

'Hey!' he said, stopping in front of them, staring directly at Piper.

'Hi,' she said.

She couldn't think. Her brain was a complete blank and she had no idea what her face was doing – it felt frozen. She'd known she was going to see him, so why hadn't she had the foresight to come up with some devastating opening line? She tried to mentally Power Pose, but it didn't help. And Rob had looked away.

'Maxine.' He gripped her by her upper arms and went in for double cheek kisses. Piper braced herself for the same, but instead he wrapped both arms around her and squeezed lightly, mumbling, 'It's so good to see you' into her hair.

'You too,' she said into his chest. He smelled delicious, smoky and warm.

When they pulled away, Piper felt flustered, like her hair was all over the place, lipstick smeared, smoky eye turned panda-ish.

Her breath was caught somewhere behind her breastbone. This was ridiculous. She shouldn't have come.

'Good to see you both,' Maxine said and then winked – actually winked – at Piper. 'I'm going to go and…' She waved her hand to suggest mingling and Piper noticed more people had arrived. She could see Mel over by the window and the back of someone she thought was probably Dawn talking to the DJ.

'You look amazing,' Rob said, looking her up and down.

'Oh pfft,' Piper said. Even though she did look amazing. She knew she did.

Rob grinned. His teeth were straight. He'd had a brace when they were kids. One of those double-track ones.

'You look good too,' Piper said. She took a breath. That was almost a sentence. She tried for more. 'Nice suit.'

'Interviews and weddings,' he said, shooting his cuffs.

'Nice.' Her mind was blank again. Had she ever seen Rob in a suit before? She couldn't think when she would have done. School uniform didn't count. Although he had always looked good in it.

'Can I get you a drink?' he said to her enormous relief, since she'd just been thinking about him in school uniform – *what the fuck*?

'I just got one actually,' she said. 'Can I get you one?'

'No you're good. What are you having?'

'I really don't need—'

He gave her a look. And it was a look she remembered from ten years earlier. It was a look that meant this is what's happening – are you in? It was the look he'd given her when they'd sneaked into the golf club party Rob had overheard Mr Young, their Geography teacher, talking about: incredible buffet, free booze. They'd got so hammered that Piper had dared Robbie to streak across the golf course, which he'd done, inevitably, and then she'd thrown up in a bunker. For a while, there was a grainy CCTV photo of the two of them on the wall in reception. It was the look he'd given her when he'd told her his aunt had adopted two horses and invited him to come and ride them. Well, he'd told Piper they were going to feed and groom them at first, but when they'd got there – some strange smallholding off the side of the dual carriageway – his aunt had saddles and helmets ready for them and seemed to have no idea Piper had never even been near a horse, let alone ridden one. (It had been so much fun. Rob, it turned out, had been riding since he was a child, but Piper's arse had been murder for almost a week after.)

'I can't get drunk,' Piper said now. 'I've already had too much.'

Rob just smiled at her. 'Of course you can. You have to, in fact. It's a school reunion. The only way to get through these things is hammered.'

Piper shook her head. 'You haven't changed at all.'

'Nor have you,' Rob said, smiling at her. He looked fond. And appreciative. It made the hairs on Piper's arms stand on end.

'I just need to go and—' she said, waving towards the dancefloor like Maxine had done. 'Back in a min.'

'I'll come and find you,' Rob said. 'We should probably mingle. A bit.'

As she crossed the dancefloor, towards the big window where she could see the sky had darkened to a deep blue streaked with pink, Piper resisted the urge to look back. If Rob was watching her, it would be distracting. And if he wasn't, it would be disappointing. She made sure to swing her hips a little. Just in case.

CHAPTER FOURTEEN

'So have you two kept in touch then?' Mel asked, nodding towards Rob.

'Hello, Mel,' Piper said, sarcastically. 'How are you? Good to see you!'

'Sorry.' Mel grinned wryly. 'How are you? Good to see you. I saw you on *Hey, UK!* You were really good. That other woman was a right stuck-up bitch.'

Piper sat down next to her old friend. She looked, like she had on Facebook, basically the same.

'She was okay really,' Piper said.

She had no idea why she felt the need to defend Naomi Jones. She hadn't been particularly nice to Piper and the article she'd written had been vile.

'Did she believe it all?' Mel asked. 'Or was she just trying to be Katie Hopkins or something?'

'I don't know,' Piper said. 'I didn't really talk to her.'

'Did you talk to that chef?' Mel asked. 'He was hot.'

'Little bit,' Piper said. But she didn't get to give Mel any details, sparse as they were, because Rob arrived with their drinks. Noticing Piper had one already, he put hers down on the table in front of the window and held out his own glass.

'To reunions!'

'To reunions,' Piper and Mel echoed, clinking their glasses.

'And to Piper finally making it home,' Mel said. 'We going to the Magazines after this?'

Piper laughed. 'Aren't we still barred?'

'Under new management,' Mel said. 'You're fine.'

'Is that why you moved away?' Rob said. 'Cos you were barred from all the pubs on the Wirral?'

'And whose fault was that?' Piper asked.

'You never got in trouble anyway,' Mel said. 'You always left before it all kicked off. 'Goody two shoes.''

Piper shook her head, even though it was true and they all knew it. She'd never been able to understand how her friends didn't seem to mind getting into trouble. Piper had never wanted to let anyone down. Still didn't. But she always seemed to manage it anyway.

'Have you seen Dawn?' Mel asked.

'Not yet,' Piper said.

Mel nodded towards the door and when Piper looked over she saw Dawn – an enormously pregnant Dawn – heading towards them.

'Oh my god!' Piper said. 'Dawn!'

'I know.' Dawn shook her head, sending her tassel earrings swinging. 'I'm like the size of a fucking house.'

'When are you due?!'

'Not even soon,' Dawn said, sitting down on Mel's other side. 'It's twins.'

'Holy shit.'

'I know.'

'You'll be fine,' Mel said. 'You'll be amazing.'

'I'm trying to talk my mum into taking one off me,' Dawn said. 'We could alternate them maybe.'

Piper grinned at her. She was the same. Exactly the same.

'Like, I didn't think I'd be able to look after one. I can't fucking believe I'm going to have to look after two. I went to an antenatal class the other day and the woman was talking about me feeding them both at the same time, like... one under each arm? And I was like "fuck that noise". Can you imagine? I'm not a milking machine. I'll do them one at a time or not at all.' She looked Rob up and down. 'Sorry to launch straight into tit chat.'

Rob shrugged, smiling. 'It's fine.'

'I won't tell you about the state of my nipples though. Save that for later. And I can't even have a fucking drink. Jesus.'

Rob left to get Dawn a J2O and the three of them looked at each other. The DJ was playing 'Uptown Funk', but it wasn't yet loud enough to interfere with conversation, the dancefloor was still empty.

'I was trying to remember when you were last home,' Dawn said to Piper. 'Since… you know.'

Before Piper's parents died, she meant.

'I've been home,' Piper said. 'But I usually just stay one night and don't go out or anything.'

'Where d'you stay?' Dawn asked.

'With my Aunty Connie.'

'Fuck me, is she still alive?!'

Mel spat out a mouthful of beer, snorting with laughter and wiping her chin with the back of her hand. 'Jesus, Dawn. You don't change, do you?'

'Sorry,' Dawn said. 'But wasn't she dead old when you lived here?'

'She's eighty-three,' Piper said.

'And she's your aunty? I always thought she was your nan.'

'No, my grandparents died ages ago,' Piper said. It wasn't quite that simple, but she wasn't going to get into it. 'And she's actually my great-aunt. She's my mum's aunt.'

'Ah right,' Dawn said. 'I was dead sorry, you know. About your mum and dad. They were lovely.'

Piper had known this would happen – how could it not – but she had to swallow hard and blink tears back anyway. Sometimes it was fine and she could talk about it, but other times…

'Sorry,' Dawn said, reaching over and squeezing Piper's knee. 'I didn't mean to upset you. Do you want me to tell you about my piles? Take your mind off it.'

'I'd rather talk about my dead parents,' Piper managed to squeak out and Mel and Dawn laughed.

A tear spilled anyway and Piper wiped it with her fingertips, turning to look out of the window at the fort and the river. For so long – for years, since she'd left really – she'd wondered what it would be like to be home, to hang out with her friends again. She thought they'd resent her for leaving the way she had. She thought at the very least they wouldn't want to spend any time with her. But this felt the same as it always had. This felt like nothing had changed at all. It was nice. But also a little disconcerting. She'd spent years trying to become a different person, to leave the old Piper behind. If she'd succeeded – and she'd thought she had – how come she could fit back in so easily?

Rob pulled a chair over and sat just in front of them. He leaned back and crossed one ankle over the other knee and Piper felt a bit stunned at how much like an actual adult he looked.

'What?' he said, looking back at her.

'Oh god.' She laughed. 'You just look like such a grown-up! It's weird.'

'Me? Dawn's creating new humans.'

'Yeah, but she looks pretty much the same,' Piper said.

'And she sounds exactly the same,' Mel agreed.

'But you used to be skinny and, like, a teenage boy and now you're like—'

'A maaaaaaaan,' Dawn said dramatically.

Piper laughed. 'Right.'

'He wasn't this hot at school, was he?' Dawn said, looking at the other women.

Rob laughed, ducking his head, rubbing one hand over the back of his neck.

'He was,' Mel said, glancing at Piper. 'Well, maybe not this hot. But hot. Wasn't he, Piper?'

Piper blinked at her. She couldn't even look at Rob.

'I don't know,' she lied. 'I always thought he was a massive dork.'

'I was definitely a massive dork,' Rob said.

'Seriously though,' Dawn said. 'Do you, like, work out or something?'

Mel shrieked with laughter. 'Was that meant to be a pick-up line? Because this really isn't a good time.'

'Oh give me a break,' Dawn said. 'I haven't had sex for six months. Carl can't get near me with this.' She gestured at her enormous belly. 'And he doesn't want to anyway. Do you know what he said? "What if I hurt the baby's head?" I said, "Don't flatter yourself."' She rolled her eyes. 'But the hormones give me the right horn. Pregnancy is bullshit.'

'You remember when we used to tell you you needed more male friends?' Mel told Rob. 'This is why.'

'I've got male friends!' Rob said. 'I had male friends back then too.'

'Yeah, like two of them,' Mel said.

'So?' Dawn said. 'What do you do then? I'm going to need a personal trainer cos by the time I get these buggers out I'll be a right fat bitch.'

Piper's face felt hot. She forced herself not to react. Dawn didn't seem to even think about it.

'I used to go to the gym,' Rob said. He shifted his leg, pressing his knee against Piper's. She looked at him, surprised, but he was still looking over at Dawn. 'But I mostly just run now,' he finished.

'Oh yeah,' Mel said. 'I remember seeing that on Facebook. You did that muddy one.'

'And an Iron Man!' Dawn said, sitting up straight and bracing her arms against her knees. 'I remember seeing it now. Cos I remember wondering then how you'd got so big.'

'Jesus,' Mel said. 'Keep it in your pants.'

'Yeah,' Rob said. 'I did an Iron Man a couple of years ago. Wouldn't do that again though, it was too fucking hard.'

Mel snorted.

'The Tough Mudder was okay. I'm not bothered about anything like that though really. That was just what I did to make myself keep running. I do it automatically now. Feels weird if I don't.'

'I don't do anything like that,' Mel said. 'I've got a step counter on my phone and if I've got the day off work the only steps I do are between the sofa and the fridge.'

'Where do you work?' Piper asked Mel. She was relieved to be able to change the subject. The thought of Rob running, or Rob covered in mud, or Rob doing whatever you did in an Iron Man – swimming? Cycling? Rolling tyres and pulling trucks? – was making her flustered. Not to mention the fact that he'd noticed Dawn's casual fatphobia and had made a point of letting Piper know he had.

'Wetherspoons,' Mel said. 'Just along the front there. I'm Assistant Bar Manager. Been there since it opened.'

'Do you like it?' Piper asked.

'It's a good laugh,' Mel said, shrugging. 'What about you?'

While Piper told Mel about her job, Dawn was asking Rob about his. Piper wanted to listen – she realised she still couldn't believe he was a teacher – but she couldn't do that and talk to Mel at the same time. Every time she let her eyes drift over in his direction, she'd look back to find Mel looking smug. She'd never told Mel she'd fancied Rob when they were teens, but she was sure she knew. Mel always knew everything about everyone. She was one of those people.

'Ooh!' she said suddenly. 'I love this song!'

Piper glanced over her shoulder and was surprised to find that while they'd been talking a few people had actually started dancing.

'Come on, Rob,' Mel said, grabbing his hand as she passed Piper.

Rob let himself be pulled onto the dancefloor.

CHAPTER FIFTEEN

Piper heard Claire before she saw her and immediately felt fifteen again. She could feel her shoulders starting to curl, her belly fluttering with nerves. But she wasn't fifteen any more and Claire couldn't do anything to her now. (Her brain immediately started suggesting the many and varied things Claire could do to her, from knocking her off her chair to that bucket of blood she'd discussed with Matt, but even she knew they were pretty unlikely. At worst, she'd blank her.)

Piper straightened up, pulling her shoulders back, and looked over at Dawn, who was rolling her eyes.

'Who's she with?' Piper mouthed.

'Lauren,' Dawn said, not even bothering to lower her voice. They probably wouldn't hear over the music, but still.

Piper really wanted to turn round and look. Claire and Lauren had been inseparable at school. Claire had been the leader and Lauren basically her henchwoman and she couldn't quite believe they were still at it now. But maybe they weren't. Maybe they'd changed completely and were embarrassed when they looked back.

'Piper!' Claire said, from just behind Piper's shoulder. 'I didn't know you were going to be here!'

Piper turned and looked up at her teen nemesis. She looked basically the same, just more polished. Her hair was glossier and clearly professionally highlighted rather than home-dyed. She'd been a fake tan addict at school and while she now had a healthy glow, she wasn't orange. Her smile still didn't reach her eyes.

'You look well,' she said.

Paige almost laughed. 'Thanks. You too.'

'I saw you on breakfast TV. I couldn't believe it was you. I'd never do something like that, but good for you.' She looked Piper up and down and Piper stared back at her, holding her breath.

'Rob's here,' Lauren said and Piper looked away from Claire to look at Lauren. She'd hardly changed at all: still too blonde, too tanned, her dress too tight, like a copy of Claire with the wrong filter.

'Yeah, he's sitting there actually,' Dawn said, pointing at the seat next to Piper. 'So you should probably…'

Claire looked over at Dawn and laughed out loud. 'Bloody hell. You look like you're about to burst.'

'Another good reason for you to get out of the way,' Dawn said.

Piper stared at her. Dawn had been the same at school. She just didn't give a fuck. Piper had both admired her and been intimidated by her. She remembered Dawn having a go at her once – they were on the mossy rocks in front of Vale Park, she thought, though she couldn't think why they would have been down there. Dawn had told her to worry less about what people thought of her. All it had done was make Piper worry what Dawn had thought of her.

'Nice to see you anyway,' Claire said. 'I saw your Carl the other night in the Ship. He was talking to that barmaid, you know the bulimic one?' She did a sad head tilt.

*

'Still a cow,' Dawn said, as soon as Claire and Lauren had gone. 'Pair of cows. You'd think they'd have grown out of it by now.'

Piper smiled. So far everyone she'd met had been pretty similar to who they'd been at school. But she wasn't. Was she? She'd worked really hard not to be.

*

Claire had known Piper liked Rob. Piper didn't know how she knew because she worked really hard to hide it and thought she'd succeeded. But then one day, they'd been in the park, sitting on the edge of the bandstand, while the boys played football on the grass. Claire had been smoking and Piper had been wondering whether she should ask to try or whether that would just lead to humiliation. And why did she even want to try anyway? Just to fit in with the other girls? Or because she was bad at trying anything new and really bad at doing anything bad?

'He'd never go out with you, you know,' Claire had said.

Piper's stomach had dropped immediately. Like it did when her mum drove too quickly over the railway bridge on the way to the big Tesco.

'What?' Piper had said, before she'd had a chance to think better of it.

'Robbie,' Claire said, leaning forward, her elbows on her knees and looking past Lauren to Piper. Mel had gone to join in the football 'for feminism' and Dawn had already gone home to look after her little step-brother. 'He would never go out with you. So there's no point in fucking gazing at him all the time.'

'I wasn't,' Piper said. And she didn't think she had been. She was just watching them play football. Not just Robbie. Sam and Mark and Mel. Robbie had just stopped and pulled his jumper over his head and she'd looked then because sometimes his T-shirt came up too and revealed a strip of his stomach, but apart from that… she definitely hadn't been staring. She didn't think.

'Maybe if you lost some weight,' Claire said.

And even though Piper had known it was coming – it had been inevitable – she still felt like she'd been punched.

'I don't—' Piper tried.

'He's nice to everyone, Robbie,' Claire continued. She wasn't looking at Piper any more – she was watching the boys and Mel. 'But you really shouldn't think that you have a chance. Because there's just no way. So I don't want you to embarrass yourself. You know, more than you already have.'

Lauren laughed.

Piper looked at her feet, dangling in front of the bandstand. At her new silver glitter Converse. She knew Claire was just being a bitch. She was like that literally all the time – everyone knew it. Piper wasn't sure why they still tolerated her hanging out with them, but she just always seemed to turn up. She watched her feet and thought about moving away and never having to see or talk to Claire ever again. She couldn't wait.

*

By the time the buffet was uncovered, everyone but Dawn was pretty drunk. The DJ had switched from current hits to noughties classics and everyone (again, apart from Dawn, who was sitting in the window seat, alternately scrolling her phone and filming everyone for Snapchat) was up dancing.

Claire had been dancing with Rob for a while, so Piper danced with Mel and Maxine and anyone else who danced over to them. Mel was incapable – had always been incapable – of dancing seriously, so she was busy making up little routines and nudging Piper to get her to join in. At one point, Piper found herself dancing with Miss Crowley's boyfriend, his hands on her hips, his mouth up against her ear while he tried to say something Piper couldn't hear over the music.

Over his shoulder she saw Rob watching them, his eyebrows pulled together in a frown. Claire was yelling something up at him, her face bright, but he didn't seem to have noticed. The next time Piper turned around, Claire had gone and Rob was right behind her, reaching for her hand. She held it out and let him take it and then he was twirling her under his arm and she staggered on her heels, remembering that she'd been planning to take them off, had intended to bring a pair of Converse with her for later, but then she'd forgotten all about it.

The song ended and Rob was holding her hand and pulling her across the dancefloor again. She entertained a short fantasy about going to the bathroom and straddling him on the loo, but then they were back at the buffet and he was pulling a breadstick out of a pot like he was picking straws. She had no idea where Miss Crowley's boyfriend had gone.

'I thought we could dance and then eat and then dance!' he said. He looked so proud of his plan that Piper started laughing again. She'd laughed more tonight than she could remember laughing for a long time.

'Oh fuck,' Rob said.

The breadstick was sticking out of the corner of his mouth like a cigar and Piper wanted to poke it with her finger. Or steal and eat it. Where was her drink?

'What?'

But then she realised. 'Sex on Fire'.

'This is sick and wrong,' Rob said.

Their teachers – Mr Rogers, the history teacher; Mr Davis, geography; Mrs Chipchase, French –were all dancing, gyrating and singing along with 'Sex on Fire'.

'It's a good job Mr Rich isn't here,' Piper said. 'Sexy beast.'

Rob rolled his eyes at her. She grabbed a sandwich and hobbled over to the window to find her drink.

'You okay?' she asked Dawn, who'd pulled one of the chairs over and had her feet up on it. 'Need anything?'

'I need to get these fucking babies out, but other than that… Is there any chicken legs left?'

By the time Piper had got Dawn chicken legs and another drink for both of them, Rob was dancing again.

'Come and dance with me!' he yelled at Piper.

It was the Arctic Monkeys. 'I Bet You Look Good on the Dancefloor'.

As Piper headed over to Rob, she remembered him singing it on the prom one night years ago – standing on a bench, head thrown back. The rest of them had thrown chips at him and eventually a seagull swooped down to steal them and Rob acted as if it was a fan, badgering him for an autograph. He'd had a half-decent voice too. Piper had even thought his band might actually do something. If they'd spent more time rehearsing/ playing and less time messing around/drinking.

'Stop thinking,' Rob said, his mouth near her ear, his arms around her. She leaned back against him and tried not to pretend he was her boyfriend, that she still lived here, that this was her actual life.

She turned in his arms and grinned, singing along with the song.

*

Piper was exactly at the point of drunk where she absolutely should stop drinking, but probably wouldn't. She'd had a couple of glasses of water and eaten a couple of sandwiches and a chicken leg from the buffet and now she was more interested in dancing than drinking.

'They just brought out a bowl of crackling!' Rob yelled directly into her ear.

'What?'

'Crackling! Proper crackling!'

He seemed so excited that she let him tug her back over to the buffet table where he presented a metal bowl of crispy stuff as if it was some sort of treasure.

'It's pork scratching?' Piper said, peering into the bowl.

'Oh my god,' Rob said. 'No.'

He popped a piece of crackling directly into her mouth and she giggled before saying, 'Oh my god.'

'I know! I haven't had proper crackling for ages. It's the best.'

'Oh my god.' It was crunchy and also soft and salty and a bit sweet and it might have been the best thing Piper had ever tasted in her life.

'It'll go quick,' Rob said. 'Should we hide it?'

He looked so earnest that Piper started to laugh, covering her mouth with her hand. After a couple of seconds, Rob started too. He'd taken his jacket off earlier, hanging it over the back of his chair, and at some point since he'd also undone his cuffs and rolled up the sleeves of his white shirt. His forearms were golden brown and brushed with dark hair. Piper couldn't stop looking at them.

'Shit, no. We can't hide it.' He glanced around. 'What can we do?'

Piper picked up another piece and bit the end off, groaning again at the deliciousness. 'I cannot believe I've never had this before.'

A cheer went up from everyone on the dance floor and Piper spotted Rob's resultant grin before she realised what the song was: 'Mr Brightside'. Of course it was.

Rob wrapped his hand around her wrist and pulled her out into the middle of the crowd. Everyone seemed to be losing their minds, jumping up and down with their arms around each other. Rob wrapped one arm around her waist and swung her around. She dipped her head back and looked up at the lights on the ceiling. They were soft and out of focus, leaping around and blurring. She was so drunk.

Rob grabbed her hand, his other hand on her waist and the two of them rocked from side to side, both singing. Rob was a surprisingly good dancer, she thought. Or maybe it was just that everyone was drunk and terrible.

Along with everyone else, Rob was yelling the lyrics and Piper stared at his mouth as he sang that it was only a kiss. She wondered what it would be like to kiss him. She'd always wondered. She'd wondered for years. Maybe she should just do it. Except she shouldn't because her friends were here. Teachers were here. Plus she was drunk. And she'd just eaten a bunch of crackling. She laughed instead. She couldn't believe she hadn't wanted to come. It had been the best night she'd had for ages.

CHAPTER SIXTEEN

'Oh sweet Jesus, my head,' Piper groaned. Or tried to. Her voice didn't quite manage to escape her throat.

'I made you a tea,' Rob said gently.

Piper yelped. Rob. What the fuck?

'Oh god,' she murmured. 'What the fuck?'

'There's a bucket next to the bed if you… you know.'

Piper curled on her side, pressing her face into the pillow. Her head was throbbing , her stomach churning, but worse than that was the shame. What had she done last night? Flashes of memory were trying to push their way to the front of her mind, but she wasn't ready for that yet. Maybe she never would be. Could you book yourself in for a lobotomy? Had no one made *Eternal Sunshine*-style memory wiping real yet? They should get on that.

'Can I get you anything?' Rob said.

He sounded near, but Piper didn't think he was actually in the bed with her. She slid her foot across the sheet. No, she was definitely the only one in the bed.

'I can do a fry-up?' Rob said.

Piper wanted to pull the duvet up over her head and wait for death. Instead she forced one eye open and focussed it on the mug of tea on the bedside table.

'I think just tea is good for now. Thanks.'

'Okay,' Rob said. 'I'm going to go down to Morrisons and get bacon and eggs anyway. In case you change your mind. And sausage? Do you like black pudding?'

Piper's stomach roiled.

'I'll just get the stuff and you can see what you feel like later. Okay?'

'Great,' Piper murmured. 'Thank you.'

*

Once Rob had gone, not just out of the room, but out of the flat – Piper waited to hear the front door click closed – she dragged herself slowly to sitting and blinked both eyes open. Rob's bedroom. In Rob's flat. Grown-up Rob. She'd been in Rob's bedroom a couple of times when they were teens. It had been a typical teen boy's bedroom: smelled like socks, clothes on the floor, posters on the walls, mugs and dishes and abandoned towels everywhere. He had a TV and some game console – she couldn't remember what – and she'd been envious because she wasn't allowed technology in her room. She'd been fascinated by it all: the bed Rob slept in, where he took his clothes off and put his clothes on. Where he no doubt watched porn and wanked. She hadn't been able to think about that for too long, the butterflies in her belly overwhelming her.

Grown-up Rob's room – she really had to stop thinking of him as 'grown-up Rob' –was tidy, apart from a pile of trainers and shoes under the window. The walls were grey and plain apart from a framed poster above the bed. Piper was too hungover to tip her head back enough to see what it was. There was a pile of books on the other bedside table, next to a pint glass of water and a set of earbuds. And her dress – her silver sequinned kimono dress – was draped over a chair in the corner, her bag and shoes on the floor underneath. Had Rob undressed her? She was wearing her underwear, thank god, but… surely Rob hadn't undressed her? She cringed, lying back down again and pressing both hands to her face. Why? Why had she got so drunk? She'd promised herself she wouldn't. She was meant to be coming home and showing everyone that she'd been right to leave, that she had a whole different life now. Instead she'd immediately become a drunken mess. Matt would piss himself when she told him.

Piper forced herself to drink half the mug of tea before carefully clambering out of bed and padding across the room to the chair. She opened her bag to get her phone and yelped at the sight and the smell. Why was her bag full of pork scratchings?

Back on the bed, she texted Matt: *Got hammered. Woke up in Rob's bed. Kill me.*

The phone rang almost immediately and Piper jumped, before clutching her head with her free hand.

'Ow,' she said when she answered.

'Get it girl,' Matt said. She could hear him laughing. She hated him.

'I hate you.'

'So. How was it?'

'We didn't have sex.'

'Blowie? Handie? Did he just focus on your neeeeeds?'

'Nothing? I don't think? I think we might've kissed, but also that could've been a dream.'

'Where is he now? Are you still at his place?'

Piper rubbed the back of her neck. It felt crunchy. Like crackling.

'He's gone to get bacon and eggs. He's going to make breakfast.'

'I feel like you definitely must've shagged him. Unless he thinks the fry-up'll make you put out.'

'I definitely didn't shag him. It's been a while. I'd know.'

'That's good anyway. That he didn't take advantage of you in your delicate condition.'

'That's pregnancy. And I think it's pretty basic not to shag someone when they're drunk.'

'Oh fucking hell, Pipes, not too hungover for a feminist lecture, eh? I know. I was joking. Are you okay?'

'I feel like I'm dying. And I'm kind of cool with it.'

He laughed. 'The fry-up'll help, I promise.'

'I'll have to talk to him. What if I said stuff last night?'

'What kind of stuff? Like about his arms and his jaw and his full bottom lip and deep blue eyes?'

Piper groaned. 'Oh what the fuck?'

'You texted me,' Matt said. He was so smug. 'You tried to send me a photo of him, but it was blurry as fuck. So you described him instead. He sounds hot. Almost gave *me* the horn, never mind you.'

'Oh god.' She drank the rest of her tea. It helped. A little.

'Don't worry about it,' Matt said. 'I've been around you drunk loads of times. You talk a fuck of a lot, but you never do anything properly embarrassing. Not like Jodie.'

Jodie was prone to taking her clothes off when drunk. All of them. And once, they'd all left a club – one of the few times Piper had gone out with Matt and his friends – and Jodie had disappeared down an alley for a wee, then fallen over backwards with her knickers round her ankles, and just lay there, howling with laughter, until the rest of them had gone to find her. She wasn't even embarrassed the next day. In fact, she kept recreating it to make the rest of them laugh.

'You probably told him you'd missed him at the very worst,' Matt said. 'That's all. I promise.'

'I don't know,' Piper said. 'What if I, like…'

'Told him you want to climb him like a tree?'

'Oh god.'

'He might be into it.'

'He won't be. He never was.'

'You don't know that. How far away is the supermarket?'

'What supermarket?'

'The one he's gone to to get breakfast things. Which, by the way, isn't something men do for women they don't like.'

'He's just nice. He was always nice.'

'You're such an idiot. How far is it?'

'Ten minutes maybe?'

'So get your arse out of bed and make yourself presentable for when he gets back. You've probably got make-up all over your face and hair like a bonfire.'

'Fuck,' Piper said. 'I'll ring you later.'

'Send me another photo of him. See if you can get a shirtless one.'

'Thank you,' Piper said, swinging her legs out of bed and taking a moment to allow her stomach to settle.

'No probs. Love you.'

'Love you too.'

Piper took a few deep breaths before standing and shuffling over to the bedroom door. But when she opened it, she was relieved to find it was actually an en-suite bathroom. Bright and clean and smelling like lemons. Perfect.

CHAPTER SEVENTEEN

'You're up!' Rob said, coming through the door with a Morrisons carrier bag in each hand. 'How are you feeling?'

'Bit… rough,' Piper said.

She'd shrieked at her reflection in the bathroom mirror. As Matt had predicted, her make-up had been smeared black around her eyes, her hair flat on one side and standing straight up on the other. But she'd stood under a hot shower for a while, moaning gently, and felt much better for it. Well, not much. But better. Putting on the previous night's clothes hadn't felt great, but it wasn't as if she had any alternative. And then she'd sat very still on the sofa in Rob's open plan living room/diner and waited for him to come back.

'You could've gone outside,' Rob said, crossing the room behind her to the kitchen. 'It's a nice day.'

'Out where?' Piper asked.

Rob crossed the room and pulled back the hazy white curtains. They slid smoothly open to reveal a wall of windows, overlooking the river, the beach and the fort.

'Bloody hell.' Piper pushed herself up to standing with the arm of the sofa. 'I had no idea.'

Rob grinned at her. 'You saw it last night. The curtains were open when we came back. You kept saying how gorgeous it was. I slept on the sofa, by the way. In case you were worried.'

'Ugh, god.' She crossed the room and stood next to him at the window, squinting against the sun. 'Sorry. Was I a total dick?'

'No!' He quickly squeezed her upper arm before letting go. Piper could still feel the heat of his hand. 'You were lovely. Funny.'

He pulled a handle and slid one of the doors open. Fresh cold air rushed into the flat.

'You can sit out there, if you want? While I make breakfast? Or you can stay inside? Up to you.'

'Um,' Piper said. 'Outside, I think?' The sea air was already making her head feel clearer.

'I'll bring you another tea out.'

Piper stepped out onto the balcony and over to the frosted glass panels, leaning her elbows on the top and resting her head in her hands, massaging her temples with the tips of her fingers. She watched seagulls swoop down on the beach and a small dog running and chasing a ball. The cranes over in the docks in Liverpool were still but the wind turbines were spinning slowly.

Why had she got so drunk? She knew why. Because she'd been nervous. Of seeing Rob. Of seeing her former friends. Mel. Dawn. Claire. All of them. Because she hated coming back. Didn't want to be reminded of who she used to be. Hadn't wanted to answer questions about her parents. She winced as she remembered wiping tears from her face, someone – Mel maybe? – saying, 'She's upset. Get her another drink, Rob.' She'd cried. How embarrassing. They probably all thought she was an absolute wreck.

She rolled her shoulders back. It was fine. She didn't have to see them again after this weekend. She was going back to London. To her flat and her job and her friends. To the life she'd fantasised about when she'd lived here. To the life she'd never really believed she'd get to have. That she was sure her friends didn't believe she'd get to have. To the life she wouldn't have if her parents hadn't died.

'You don't have sugar, right?' Rob said, bringing another tea through. 'I don't, so I didn't even think until after I left earlier.'

'No,' Piper said, turning and smiling at him, as he put the mug of tea down on the table. 'Just milk, no sugar.'

'Didn't think so. How's the head?'

'Getting better. I've just the shame to deal with now.'

'Oh fuck that noise,' Rob said. 'Everyone gets pissed. And I told you, you were fine.'

'Was I singing Elbow?' She'd had 'One Day Like This' stuck in her head since she'd woken up.

He laughed. 'We all were. It was great. I'd better get back to the breakfast.'

He went back inside. Piper could smell the bacon and her stomach gave a pitiful grumble, like it was willing to attempt food, but it wasn't making any promises. She sat down on one of the comfy chairs and closed her eyes, turning her face up to the sun. Another memory appeared: she was bent double laughing on the dancefloor. She couldn't think who she'd been dancing with – everything was a blur and flashing lights. And then… had she been talking to one of her teachers? Mr Rogers? He'd been one of her favourite teachers actually. Had he really been there? Or was that bit a dream?

Rob called out that breakfast was ready and Piper went inside, taking her tea with her.

'Was Mr Rogers there last night?' she asked. She spotted the food on the table. 'This looks amazing, Rob, god.'

'Sit down,' Rob said. 'You're fine. And yeah, he was there. You were very excited to see him.'

'Oh god. I didn't try to kiss him or anything, did I?' She sat down, thinking *I didn't try to kiss you?*

Rob snorted. 'Not that I saw, no. I think you were just telling him he was your favourite. I remember you talking about weeing on leather? And bread for plates? Something like that.'

Piper shook her head. 'Literally all I remember from history. And he taught me that.'

'I remember crop rotation,' Rob said. 'Feel like that's all we learned for years. I don't think any crops need that much rotation.'

Piper cut into one of the two sausages on her plate and tentatively raised it to her mouth. 'Now if this makes me sick it's because of my own choices and not a comment on your cooking, okay?'

Rob smiled. 'Noted.'

As soon as Piper swallowed the first bite of sausage she felt better. 'God, Rob. Thank you for doing this. I really appreciate it.'

'No worries. You were pretty insistent that you couldn't go back to your aunt's last night.'

'Shit!' Piper said, dropping her fork – it clanged against the edge of her plate. 'Did I phone her? She'll be worried sick.'

She started shoving her chair back, but stopped when Rob held a hand up and said, 'No, you're fine. You definitely rang her. I heard you.'

'Shit,' Piper said. 'Thank you. God, I can't believe it took me this long to even think about her.'

'Makes sense,' Rob said, shrugging. 'You don't usually have to.'

'I guess,' Piper said. 'Bloody hell.'

'You said she'd kick off if you went back drunk.'

Piper smiled. 'She wouldn't kick off. But she'd make little comments about it for the rest of my life. I was drunk once at her house years ago. I was fifteen or something? I was probably with you actually! In Central Park?'

'Oh god, yeah. Was it cider? Jess brought loads of…'

'Strongbow,' they both said at the same time.

'My parents were away,' Piper said. 'So I was staying with Aunty Connie. But we all went to the park and then I went back to hers thinking there was no way she'd know. Course she knew right away.'

'We got picked up by the police,' Rob said.

'Oh shit! I'd forgotten that!'

'I was asleep. Literally woke up with a policeman leaning over me. I was grounded for weeks.'

Piper laughed. 'I remember you messaging me about it. I wanted to come and sneak in your window like on *Dawson's Creek* or something.'

Rob swallowed some bacon and said, 'It always pissed me off that there wasn't a tree outside my window. I was desperate to escape.'

'Remember when you rescued me from that tree?' Piper said.

She hadn't actually meant to say it because it wasn't one of her most impressive memories. A bunch of them had been hanging round in the park and daring each other to climb trees. Amanda had been really good at it – she'd clambered up the trunk and then appeared at the very top, head poking through the leaves, waving at the rest of them. She was fearless. Piper could comfortably climb one – with an enormous trunk and wide branches, split to practically make seats, but there was another that everyone clambered up, leaving Piper on the ground. Jess had been taking the piss out of her, she remembered, which was what had eventually convinced her to join the rest of them. She'd shuffled along the branch and it was only when she was quite far out that she realised she'd have to jump down. And she'd frozen. She hadn't been able to move at all, not even shuffle back to the main part of the tree. She'd just sat there, gripping the branch with her nails digging in, mentally picturing herself falling off backwards and cracking her head on the ground. It hadn't even been that high. She'd just panicked.

Carl had started bouncing on the end of the branch to scare her, but Rob had shouted at him to knock it off. Piper wasn't sure if he'd spotted the tears pricking her eyes or if he was just being nice anyway, but she'd appreciated it. Rob had never been as much of a dick as the other boys. He could be loud and stupid and lairy, same as the rest of them, but he'd always been kind, had never deliberately hurt anyone. He'd jumped down and moved until he was standing just under Piper and had held his arms up.

'I'll catch you.'

Piper had shaken her head. She was the heaviest of all of them, she knew. She knew because once at Amanda's she'd made everyone get weighed and there'd been no chance of Piper getting out of it. Going along with it had seemed easier than making everyone think she was self-conscious about it. But she knew that she weighed ten pounds more than Robbie.

'You'll get flattened,' Piper had heard Carl say.

'Fuck off, Carl,' Rob had said without even turning his head, just looking straight up at Piper.

She'd lowered herself as far as she could without actually letting go or jumping. Her arms had trembled and she'd been genuinely afraid she might wet herself, but then Robbie said, 'It's okay. Nearly there.' And she'd let go. And he hadn't even had to catch her. She'd dropped to the ground heavily, stumbled, and his hands had immediately gone to her hips to steady her.

'Okay?' he'd said.

She hadn't been able to speak – she'd just nodded.

'Ignore them,' he'd said. 'They're dickheads.'

Piper had looked at his mouth. At his soft lips. Had let herself imagine that he might like her. That maybe he'd kiss her. Not there and then in front of everyone. But one day. Maybe. Somewhere.

'I like chubby girls better anyway,' he'd said. And ruined it.

CHAPTER EIGHTEEN

When Piper got back to Aunt Connie's, she was greeted by Buster jumping up at her legs and immediately rolling onto his back, his entirely body wriggling with joy.

'Balcony!' Connie yelled from the kitchen. 'Before he pees!'

Piper grabbed the giddy dog around his middle and rushed across the room, holding him at arms' length, before depositing him on the tiny balcony where he immediately let go, a small puddle spreading across the concrete.

'Honestly, mate, keep it together,' Piper said.

He scratched at the concrete a little before trotting back inside.

'Nice,' Piper said, looking down at the puddle. It was a good job her stomach had settled. But then she had Rob to thank for that.

'Did you have a good time?' Connie said, coming through to the living room.

Piper closed one of the balcony doors and turned to look at her aunt, who was wearing the same clothes as yesterday, but with an apron over the top.

'I did, thanks,' Piper said.

'How's your head this morning?'

Piper smiled. 'Better than it was when I woke up.'

'Have you had something to eat?'

'Yes. Thanks. Rob made a cooked breakfast.'

'Robbie Kingsford? I saw his mum in the bank the other day. What's he doing now?'

Piper frowned. 'He's a teacher. At Rocklands.'

'Oh yes,' Connie said. 'I think I knew that.'

'He lives in one of those new flats on the prom.'

'Does he?' Connie gasped. 'More money than sense then.'

'It's nice. He's got a huge balcony looking out over the river.'

'I've got a balcony,' Connie said, pointing. 'It might be covered in dog wee right now, but it's nice to sit out of an evening.'

Piper smiled. 'It's lovely. The whole flat's lovely.'

'And I didn't pay over the odds for it either. Tea?'

'Please,' Piper said. She sat down on the sofa and Buster immediately jumped up on her lap and turned around a couple of times before flopping down, hot belly over Piper's thighs.

Connie brought the tea through and then went into her bedroom for another box. Piper's heart sank. She loved the ring Connie had given her, had been wearing it every day, but she knew Connie had some of her parents' stuff to show her and she wasn't sure she was ready for that. In fact, she was sure she wasn't ready.

'Now I know this is hard for you,' Connie said, lifting out a photo album, 'but it's been eight years. And I'm not going to be here forever. I would hate to think something might happen to me and all these things would be lost.'

Piper shook her head. She couldn't look at the photos – there was no way.

'You don't have to look at them now,' Connie said. 'But take this home with you and look at them when you're ready. But don't leave it too long, eh?'

'Okay,' Piper said, her voice barely more than a whisper.

'There's these too.' Connie handed her two small notebooks. Piper took them and then realised they were address books.

'Your dad's Little Black Book there!' Connie said, laughing.

Piper held her dad's book, which actually was black, up to her nose. She didn't really expect it to smell anything like him and of course it didn't, but she had to try. She opened it, but as soon as she saw his smooth round handwriting on the first page, she had to close it again. She wasn't ready.

Her mum's book was gold, the paper not dissimilar to fish scales – just holding it in her hand took her right back to sitting on the floor at her mum's feet and fishing it out of her bag to look through. She suspected it may even contain pages she'd scribbled on. But she couldn't look.

Her phone pinged with a message and she put the address books down next to her, on top of the photo album. When she got home she'd have to find somewhere to put them where she couldn't see them, but where they'd be safe until she was ready.

'Rob's going to give me a lift to the station,' she told her aunt.

'New Brighton?' She looked confused. New Brighton station was only a few minutes' walk away.

'No. Lime Street. He's going to pick me up.'

'He was always a lovely boy,' Connie said.

'Yeah,' Piper said, replying to his text. 'He still is.'

CHAPTER NINETEEN

Rob had suggested coming up to say hello to Aunt Connie (and Buster), but Piper had said he'd never get out of there if he did, so instead she headed downstairs to find him waiting in his car at the kerb.

'Connie says you've more money than sense,' Piper told him, as she opened the car door.

'Shit, sorry,' Rob said, apparently only just realising the passenger seat was a tip, covered with files and books, a McDonald's bag in the foot well. 'Let me…'

He grabbed them all and threw them in the back seat. Piper sat down.

'It was a Help to Buy thing,' Rob said, pulling his seatbelt on. 'The flat. You can tell her.'

Piper tried not to look at how his T-shirt pulled away from his collarbone. It wasn't a big car. They were sitting closer together than they had been at any point so far. She turned and put on her own seatbelt.

'Couldn't have done it otherwise.'

'I tried to sell her on the balcony,' Piper said. 'But she's got her own balcony, so that didn't even impress her.'

'She's up there now,' Rob said, pointing.

Piper looked up and saw Connie on the balcony, looking down at them, Buster wiggling with joy – or possibly the need to pee – at her feet.

'She mainly uses the balcony for Buster,' Piper said. 'He pees when he gets excited.'

'We've all been there,' Rob said, pulling away from the kerb.

Piper snorted with laughter and then covered her mouth, but Rob glanced at her, delighted, and for a second they were right back at school, grinning at each other across a classroom. Piper felt like she was falling. Or that she was still and the world was tipping away from her. She turned and looked out of the window, reaching one arm out to steady herself against the glove compartment.

Rob turned onto Victoria Road. 'Vicky Road' they'd called it when they were kids. There was a pub they'd been to a few times – one where they weren't that bothered about serving underage kids.

'It's all changed round here, right?' Rob said, turning again onto Rowson Street.

'Yeah,' Piper said, resting her head on the glass for a second before turning back to look at him. 'Loads of it's still the same though.'

They drove past the row of shops they used to go to on the way to the park and the prom. The chippy was gone, but the newsagent's was still there. It was a canopied Victorian parade and Piper always worried that she'd come home to find it demolished, but not this time.

It was weird, seeing Rob driving. He was so confident, looked so natural. Which… it was only driving. But still. And she couldn't do it. His hands were strong on the steering wheel, muscles flexing in his forearms.

'When did you learn to drive?' Piper asked.

'I got lessons for my eighteenth birthday.' He glanced at her and then back at the road. 'But I didn't pass till I was twenty. Kept putting the test off.'

'Did you pass first time?'

'Course!' He grinned. 'What about you?'

'Never had lessons. Don't need a car in London really.'

'I love it, driving.'

'Yeah?'

'Yeah. Down the motorway, music blasting out. Great when I'm stressed.'

They passed the library where Piper used to go with her mum after school and choose more books than she could even carry. And then they'd go on the playground before heading home. The library backed onto the cemetery.

'Every time we came along here, my dad would say, "Dead centre of town",' Piper said, pointing at the cemetery. 'For years I thought it really was. Like someone had measured it or he'd seen it on a map.'

Rob smiled.

'I was so pissed off when I finally got it. He thought it was bloody hilarious. I don't think he realised I'd taken it literally.'

'Are they...' Rob said. 'Your parents...'

Piper shook her head. 'No. They were cremated.' Her voice cracked slightly, even though she hadn't known it was going to. Even though she'd talked about it so many times without getting upset. Even though it had been years. But something about being home always brought it much closer to the surface than she ever usually allowed it to get.

'Sorry,' Rob said. 'I didn't mean to—'

'It's fine,' Piper said. She looked straight ahead. 'Honestly.'

'Put some music on now, if you want,' he said, gesturing at the glove compartment. 'There's CDs in there.'

'Retro,' Piper said, popping the door open.

'The car I had before this one had a tape deck. For like three years I couldn't pass a charity shop without checking to see if they had any I might listen to. For months, I only had Phil Collins's *No Jacket Required*. That thing must be in every charity shop on earth.'

'What's in there now?' Piper asked, turning the stereo on. 'Can I just hit play or will it be something embarrassing?'

'Do it,' Rob said, smiling. 'I'm not ashamed.'

Piper hit play and the car filled with 'Mr Brightside'.

'Oh my god,' Piper said, laughing.

'What? It's a banger!'

'It is. I love it. It's just exactly what I would have guessed you'd be listening to.'

'Oh yeah, it's easy for you to say that now.'

Piper laughed. 'I'm serious. It's a total late-twenties-man-driving song.'

'So what else is in there, if you're so clever?'

Piper tipped her head back so she couldn't cheat. 'Oasis. White Stripes. Kaiser Chiefs. Kings of Leon.'

'Pfft,' Rob said. 'Obviously.'

Piper pulled a handful of CDs out and shuffled through them. 'Oh Rob. Such a cliché.'

'There's more!' he said. 'I've got Lorde's new album.'

'Oh thank god. Cos it was looking like a real sausage fest for a bit there.'

Piper shuffled until she found *Melodrama* and pushed the CD into the slot. 'Green Light' started to play as Rob turned off the main road and down round the back of the shopping centre, past McDonald's and the bus stop they all used to hang around at after they'd been to McDonald's, past the pub they all got thrown out of once for being too noisy when the regulars were trying to watch the match, past the walk-in centre Piper had gone to when she'd broken her wrist in PE, and where Jim had taken Connie last month.

When the chorus kicked in, Piper noticed Rob was drumming his thumbs on the steering wheel. She had a sudden realisation.

'What happened to your band?'

Rob laughed, turning to look at her. 'Oh fucking hell. Yeah, we broke up. Artistic differences.'

'Gutted,' Piper said. 'I thought you were going to be the new Coldplay. Ooh, Coldplay! I bet you've got Coldplay in there too, haven't you?'

'Shut it,' Rob said. 'Everyone loves Coldplay.'

'Pretty sure everyone hates Coldplay, but okay.'

'I saw them in Manchester a couple of years ago – they were brilliant.'

Piper had forgotten this about Rob too. How he was so confident about what he liked and didn't care what anyone thought. Given that Piper had spent her entire teens worrying what people thought and trying to second-guess what might be acceptable to her friends, it had fascinated her. If she'd dared to say she liked something out of the ordinary, the others would have ripped the piss endlessly. But if Rob said he liked it, they just accepted it. She'd always wondered where he got that confidence from. She'd even asked him about it once and he'd said something like 'I just like what I like. I don't give a shit what anyone else thinks'. That had been utterly alien to her. Although Holly was like that too. She didn't understand why.

'Perfect Places' started playing as they pulled up to the Mersey tunnel. Piper flipped the CD over in her hand.

'It's on shuffle,' Rob said, as he dropped change into the toll machine.

'I was always scared of the tunnel when I was a kid,' Piper said, as they pulled away. 'I thought it might crack and water would come rushing in.'

'I like it,' Rob said. 'It's creepy. But the engineering's amazing.'

Piper smiled. 'Design and Technology teacher.'

Rob grinned without looking at her. 'Yep. I could tell you how they built it, but—'

'No, you're fine, thanks. I can live without knowing.'

The rest of the way through the tunnel they didn't talk, just listened to Lorde and stared ahead at the road.

'I always think of that *Friends* episode now,' Piper said, as they emerged into the light. '"The One With the Metaphorical Tunnel".'

'That was an actual tunnel,' Rob said. 'And I know that because I am a D and T teacher.'

Piper laughed. 'I know. I just mean I get it stuck in my head.'

'What's it a metaphor for? In *Friends*?'

'You know! Chandler's seeing Janice and he's worried it's getting too serious and he's got a fear of commitment, so...'

'I've never seen it,' Rob said.

'What?!'

'I mean, I've seen random bits of it cos it's always on some channel somewhere. And I know about "we were on a break" cos that's impossible to avoid. But I've never actually watched an episode.'

'Why not?'

He shrugged. 'Don't know really. No reason. I just haven't.'

'Oh my god. I think I've probably seen every episode at least ten times. I can't believe you've never watched it!'

Rob shrugged again. 'Sorry.'

Rob pulled off the main road and onto a small cobbled side street.

'So what's the tunnel?' he said.

'What?'

'You said the guy's afraid of commitment, but what's the tunnel?'

'Oh. Um. I think it's like the tunnel of love? At an amusement park? I'm not sure actually, now you've said that.'

Rob pulled into a parking space and turned off the engine. 'Much cheaper parking here.'

'Oh, let me pay for that,' Piper said. 'And the tunnel.'

'Don't be daft.' He took his seatbelt off and Piper watched for his T-shirt to pull away again. She wasn't disappointed. 'Have you got time for a coffee?'

Piper checked the time on her phone. 'Actually, I have.'

'You can get me a coffee then. And we're square.'

*

'I'd better get going,' Piper said, forty-five minutes later.

They'd sat outside the Costa on the station forecourt and they'd actually had time for two coffees – Rob had insisted on getting the second, despite Piper's protests, and he'd bought a slice of carrot cake for them to share too.

Piper shrugged her coat on and stood up, pushing her chair back.

'It's been really good to see you,' Rob said, standing too.

Piper blinked. 'God, I really shouldn't have had that last coffee. I'm buzzing.'

Rob grinned. 'Lightweight.'

'Oh I am. But at least I'll get some work done. Probably at double speed.'

They walked to Piper's platform and up to the train.

'So thanks,' Piper said. 'For everything. For letting me stay and bringing me over and getting me off my face on caffeine.'

'No problem,' Rob smiled. 'And sorry about that. Have you got some water?'

'In my bag,' Piper said.

There were a few minutes until the train departed and they both stood, smiling at each other. He was so lovely, Piper thought. She didn't know how she'd forgotten. She'd remembered how hot he was – and he was even hotter now, dear god – but she'd forgotten what a genuinely sweet person he was. What else had she forgotten about her other friends, her old life?

'You'd better get on then,' Rob said. 'I know I've said it already, but it really was great to see you. Again.'

He held his arms out and Piper stepped into them, smushing her face into the side of his neck. Her bag was digging into her shoulder, her nose was pressed sideways against his jaw, but she felt utterly relaxed. And safe. She felt him kiss the top of her head and she shivered.

'Let me know next time you're home, yeah?' Rob said.

'Of course,' Piper said.

They smiled at each other and then the door immediately behind her closed with a whoosh of air and she said, 'Oh shit!' and pressed the button before climbing on board. When she got to her seat, she looked up to see Rob still standing there, smiling.

She wanted to get off the train and fling herself at him, push her hands into his hair, lick his neck, bite his bottom lip. The train started pulling away. She lifted one hand and waved.

CHAPTER TWENTY

'Have you been on Facebook?' Matt said the next morning, as soon as Piper answered the phone.

'Not lately. I'm busy.' Piper was still riffling through her in-tray as she talked to Matt. Her boss was looking for the contract he'd drafted for still-called-Feminine Hygiene with notes from their lawyer, and she was sure she'd put it there, but there was no sign of it now. There'd been no sign of Lee either, which she had to admit was a relief.

'Go and look,' Matt said. Piper couldn't quite work out his tone. He sounded slightly awed, with a hint of amusement and maybe also fear.

'I can't, Matt, I'm busy. Just tell me. Is it something bad?' She gave up on the in-tray and pulled open the file drawer at the side of her desk – maybe she'd unthinkingly filed it instead?

'Rob's tagged you in a photo from the reunion.'

Piper stilled, her hands on the hanging folders, the phone cradled between her shoulder and ear.

'Is it horrible?'

'No, it's good. You're showing quite a lot of tit, but you look really gorgeous. And he looks like a fucking Greek god, Jesus. I knew he'd got hot, but—'

'Fucking hell, Matt!' she said, too loudly. Out of the corner of her eye, she saw people in the Accounts department perk up and look over at her.

'Sorry. And he's put "I said you looked good on the dancefloor" with a heart and a winky face. You need to talk to him about that.'

'So this sounds quite nice? Why are you flipping out?'

'He's checked in at a school – I assume the one he works at? And so there's loads of comments from students. About you.'

Piper's stomach felt like it was trying to escape her body. She clung to the edge of the filing cabinet. 'Fuck.'

'Yeah. You need to ring him and get him to delete it. But there's already, like, edits in the comments, so it's probably too late.'

'Fuck!' Piper said again, resting her forehead on the cabinet. It was cold. Either that or her skin was burning. 'What kind of edits?'

'They've put his face over your boobs. There's one with like a tiny version of him stuck in your cleavage.'

'Jesus Christ.'

'Piper?' John called from his office. 'Any joy?'

'I've got to go,' she told Matt. 'Thanks for telling me.'

'Okay. I'm sorry, love. Ring me in a bit.'

*

Piper only had time to text *please delete FB photo* to Rob before her boss was out of his office and bellowing at her for the contract. She spent the rest of the afternoon searching files and drawers and in-trays, along with her own bag and John's briefcase, before concluding that it was lost.

And while it wasn't her fault – probably wasn't her fault – she hated letting people down, hated anyone being annoyed with her, so John's faffing and stressing in his office while he tried to figure out if he could have actually done something with it/passed it on to someone to look at/lost it somehow stressed her right out. So she was enormously relieved to find Matt waiting for her when she left.

'I thought you might need a drink,' he said.

She smiled. 'I do. And I haven't even been on Facebook yet.'

'He deleted it,' Matt said, sliding his arm through hers and hugging her close. 'Or he untagged you, at least. I can't see if it's still on his page cos we're not friends. But…'

'But?'

'Like I said earlier, there was already screenshots and edits. It's…'

He coughed and Piper squeezed his arm. 'You can tell me. It's okay.'

'It's on LADbible.'

Piper stopped walking and stared at him. 'Oh fucking hell!'

Over the course of the afternoon, Piper hadn't been able to hold onto a single emotion for more than a couple of minutes. At first, her stomach had swooped so much that she'd genuinely thought she might be sick. Her hands had been shaking and she'd had to escape to the loo for a cry. She'd almost checked her phone then, but she knew that if she did the day would be a write-off and she'd been so sure she'd be able to find the contract –she'd never lost one before.

Searching for the contract had given her time to think and she'd told herself it didn't matter what Internet randos thought about her body. She was happy with the way she looked. And Rob apparently thought she looked good too. Not that she needed his validation. But it was nice to know he hadn't been appalled. She'd received enough shitty comments on her blog and Instagram (and Twitter and Facebook) to know that this was par for the course for the Internet. Mostly they didn't even hurt any more. So was it just because it was Rob? Because she knew Rob would have seen the comments before he made the photo private. Did she really think that knowing that other people thought she was gross would affect how he felt about her? If he felt anything beyond friendship, which probably wasn't even the case anyway.

Her brain had gone over it and over it. Round and round. Fighting between thinking that it didn't matter and that it would all be over soon, and that it was the worst thing that could possibly have happened. Becoming a body positive blogger had been an amazing thing. She was proud of herself. It had changed the way she felt about her body and herself in general. But always under the surface lingered comments that people had made in the past. The comment that Rob had made. Always just under the surface was the fear that she wasn't happy with how she looked, that she was kidding herself. That the girl who hid chocolate wrappers under her bed, the girl who would say she was too sick for a party when what she meant was that she was too fat for the clothes she'd planned to wear, the girl who had to make a joke when the boys were picking her friends up, throwing them over their shoulders and running down the beach because she knew they wouldn't be able to lift her – that that girl was still there and that this would bring her out.

*

Piper waited until she'd drunk just over half of the vodka and grapefruit Matt had insisted on buying her before she let him open Facebook and show her the photo. She was relieved that it was nice, even though she couldn't remember it being taken. She was on the dance floor and she was laughing, her head tipped back. Rob was standing behind her with his arms around her, pressing her arms to her sides, which had pushed her boobs together and given her quite ridiculously deep cleavage. He was looking at her and laughing too and he looked… fond. She ignored the tiny version of Rob stuck between her boobs.

'I know you said it didn't, but are you sure nothing happened?' Matt said. 'Between you? When you were home?'

'No!' Piper said, still staring at the photo. 'I would've told you if it had.'

'He looks like he's into you.'

He did. He really did.

'That's just Rob though,' Piper said. 'He's really friendly. And nice. And he loves his friends.'

*

'I'm so sorry,' Rob said straight away.

'It's okay,' Piper said, automatically.

She and Matt had only stayed for one drink and as soon as she'd got home she'd got into her pyjamas, poured herself another drink, and curled up on the sofa. She'd had a missed call from Rob – he must've tried when they were on the Tube – and so had called him back as soon as she was settled.

'Of course it's fucking not. Some of the comments, Pipe—'

'The comments aren't your fault.'

'No. But if I wasn't a dick who can't use Facebook properly—'

'It's just one of those things,' Piper said. 'It's not your fault. I don't know why people have to be so fucking horrible, but I can't say I'm exactly surprised. I've been getting shitty comments on my Instagram and my blog for years.'

Piper could hear Rob blowing out a breath. 'I'm sorry you have to deal with it at all,' he said. 'And I'm really sorry I made it worse. And I'm sorry I didn't get to it quicker, I was teaching and—'

'Honestly, Rob,' Piper said. 'It's fine. And it's not even really worse. Just different.'

'How are you so calm about this? I wanted to reach into the Internet and smash some heads.'

Piper laughed. 'I used to feel like that. I used to argue with people and I'd be shaking. I used to want to take screenshots and send them to their girlfriends and parents and employers, put them on a billboard, all of that. And then I read a tweet that said something like "I don't know how to explain to someone that they should care about other people" and I just thought, yeah. I could shame them into an apology. I could get them in trouble. But I can't force them to feel empathy. All I can do is carry on living my life and writing blogs and taking photos and maybe one day they'll see something and they'll get it. That's all.'

Rob was quiet for so long that Piper started to worry he'd got bored and hung up, but then she heard him blow out a breath.

'God, Pipes. You're amazing.'

'Pfft,' Piper said and then rolled her eyes at herself.

'You are,' Rob said. 'You're so strong. And kind. You always were.'

Piper laughed. She'd always tried to be kind, but she'd never thought of herself as strong.

'Shut up,' Rob said. 'You are. But I'm sorry you've had to be. And I'm sorry again for fucking up.'

*

Piper lay in the bath and thought about the comments on Rob's post. Ten years ago, they would have devastated her. Ten years ago, she was only putting tightly cropped photos online so no one would know she was fat. Or at least, she hoped that was the case. She'd felt like she was sort of okay with being fat herself, as long as no one ever commented on it. Then she'd had a period of mentioning it first, joking about it first, as if it would then hurt less when someone inevitably said something. But it hadn't. And then, slowly, eventually, she'd come to love herself.

It was hard to admit now that one of her plans for moving to London had been to lose a load of weight and then go home, looking completely different and astonishing all of her old friends. And she'd tried. She'd joined WeightWatchers as soon as she'd started uni and had a free membership at the gym, and while she frequently lost a bit of weight, she always put it back on again. She told herself university wasn't conducive to weight loss, what with the whole 'Freshman Fifteen' thing, that she couldn't actually afford decent food, didn't really know how to cook and ate most of her meals sitting at her desk working on essays. It was fine. There was plenty of time. She carried on going to the gym because she liked it – she hated the classes and the bikes, but loved the weights, swimming, the treadmill. She loved feeling worn out afterwards, loved the way her body buzzed and she slept better. Even her skin was better. So the gym plan continued, but the diets... not so much.

A few months into her first year, a boy in her seminar group asked her out. Andrew was tall – over six foot – and what her mum would have called 'well built', with fair hair and rosy cheeks. He was witty and kind and she'd already liked him, so when he suggested they go see a film at the cheap Prince Charles Cinema off Leicester Square, she'd said yes.

He'd held her hand during the film and it had been nice, his thumb stroking over the back of her hand, sending shivers up her arm and across her shoulders. Afterwards, he'd suggested going for a pizza and she'd said she couldn't, she was on a diet. He'd looked her up and down, a confused expression on his face, then he said, 'Why? You look great to me.'

She'd started to tell him how much weight she had to lose. The figures on the book she took with her for the weigh-in each week. How she had a target and she needed to lose at least a pound a week or she'd be going home in the summer still fat and she didn't want to take that chance. But she stopped herself. Because she felt great. She was wearing a black maxi dress and boots and she felt comfortable and happy and strong.

'Fuck it,' she'd said instead and they'd had the most delicious pizza and dough balls and wine and she'd laughed so much she'd spat a bit of pepperoni across the table and simply said 'Oops' rather than panicking and worrying that it would make him think she was greedy or otherwise out of control.

They'd walked back to Halls, talking the whole time and, when they found that Andrew's room-mate was still out, had sunk onto Andrew's bed. He'd stripped off her maxi dress and she'd wriggled out of her underwear, but neither of them had been able to undo the straps on the sandals so she'd kept them on while they slid their hands and lips over each other, hips pressing and legs curling, and the best thing of all, still laughing.

Afterwards, Andrew had pushed himself up against the headboard and passed Piper a bottle of water.

'That was fucking incredible,' he'd said. 'You're incredible.'

She'd kissed him just next to his nipple, rubbing her cheek against the patch of hair in the centre of his chest. She hadn't been able to speak. She hadn't known sex could be like that. She'd slept with one boy before – on their last family holiday, just before she'd left for London – and the entire experience had been hideously disappointing. But with Andrew it had been exciting and sexy and fun.

'Can we do this again some time?' he'd asked into her hair. 'Are you busy tomorrow? Next day? Day after?'

Piper had laughed. 'Next weekend?' She had an essay due.

'Hmm,' Andrew had said. 'Not sure I can wait that long.' He put the water down, flipped her over and crawled down between her legs, hooking her thighs over his shoulders.

When Andrew told her at the end of that year that he was leaving London, giving up his degree and moving back to Scotland to work for his father, she'd been upset. But not as upset as she thought she should have been. They were good friends. They'd had a good time. But they weren't in love. The main thing that she worried about was that sex would never be as good with anyone else as it had been with Andrew. And so far, it hadn't been.

She'd looked him up on Facebook not long ago when a song on the radio had reminded her of him. He was married now, with a tall, ruddy-cheeked wife, a couple of small, ruddy-cheeked children and a Rottweiler named Blue.

After her bath, lying on her bed, wrapped in a fluffy towel and with Mary Lambert on Spotify, Piper messaged Rob and asked for his address.

I've got something to send you she wrote. While she'd been looking for the contract, she'd found a CD by a band they'd signed a while ago, but whose first album had flopped badly. But Piper had loved it and thought maybe Rob would too.

Looking forward to it he replied, straight away.

CHAPTER TWENTY-ONE

At lunchtime, Piper walked up to Fulham Palace Road and bought a prawn and avocado baked potato to eat at her desk while she checked her social media.

The photo Matt had taken had more likes and comments than any photo Piper had ever posted before. At first she was worried that it had been picked up by some dickhead again, posted to Reddit with 'This is what a fat feminist looks like' or some shit. But no. It had been regrammed by a super popular BoPo blogger and featured in the Instagram story of another site Piper loved.

And for once the comments were almost entirely positive, calling her smoking hot and admiring her confidence. She felt confident just looking at the photo. She loved it. She was going to have to buy Matt a bottle of wine or something. Maybe cook him dinner.

When she opened her emails, she found she had a message from a journalist writing a piece about body positivity who wanted to interview her in person, along with a photoshoot, plus a couple of emails from brands offering her stuff to review. She'd done a bit of work with brands over the years, but the emails were from better-known companies than she'd worked with before. She made a note to get back to them as soon as she could after work. She also needed to check her PR page and make sure her terms were up to date.

After lunch, she found she had an all caps 'urgent' email about the girl band name. The list now included The Muffin Tops, Scratch That Itch, Play Nice, The Sugar Mice.

'The Sugar Mice?' Piper said out loud.

'I know, right?' someone said from further down the office.

It's a Girl Thing, The Crush, Sux, The Vacations, Eleven.

'These are all terrible,' Piper muttered, deleting the email.

She opened Facebook, intending to grab Rob's address for the padded envelope in her in-tray with the CD and card ready to send, but instead typed: *I'm going to be home this weekend. Are you around? Want to get a coffee? I could give you the thing instead of sending it.*

Once the message was sent, she shut Facebook down to ensure she didn't spend the rest of the afternoon refreshing the page.

John had left some dictation tapes in her in-tray and after she'd finished the second tape, she headed to the kitchen to make a tea and instead found three of the A&R guys, including Lee, gathered over someone's phone, snorting with laughter.

'What's up?' she said on her way past.

Instead of showing her whatever pointless video they'd been watching or saying, as the newest one, Angus, had once, 'Sorry, it's porn,' they all just stopped, perfectly still, like gazelles in a nature documentary hearing a lion approach.

'What?' Piper said, but as soon as the word was out of her mouth she knew exactly what. She took a deep breath. 'LADbible?'

Angus's eyes were wide. 'You know about it?'

She shrugged. 'Yeah. I thought the cleavage one was funny.'

She flipped the kettle on and leaned against the kitchen doorway. 'What's the big deal though? It's like these fools have never seen a woman before.'

Her heart was actually racing, but other than that she felt oddly calm. Because really, what did the picture represent apart from a fat woman having fun at a party? How was that notable?

'You look good,' Angus said, his voice coming out slightly squeaky. 'Nice... dress.'

Piper laughed. 'Thanks. It was my school reunion. Good night.'

Angus and the other guy, Phil, wandered back to their offices. Only Lee stayed behind.

'Do you, um, want to go out again? Some time?' he asked, glancing around again, his voice low.

Piper suddenly realised something. She blinked at him. 'Did we go to The Dove because you were embarrassed to be seen with me?'

'What?' he said. 'No!' His cheeks had gone pink.

'And you're asking me out again now, but whispering?'

He shook his head. 'I think you're hot and—'

'And we had nothing in common,' Piper said. 'We had an evening of awkward conversation and then an even more awkward attempt at a kiss and I really have no interest in a repeat. Thank you.'

The kettle boiled and she poured the water into the mug. When she'd finished making the tea, Lee had gone. She stayed in the kitchen while she drank her tea, thinking about how when she was a teen she would have regarded what had happened with Lee as her worst nightmare. And how now it barely mattered to her at all. Matt was right – she'd changed more than she'd let herself believe.

When she got back to her desk, there was a message from Rob: *How about I cook you dinner instead?*

CHAPTER TWENTY-TWO

'You didn't need to come,' Connie said, as soon as she opened the door. 'I'm fine.'

She looked fine. She actually looked better than the last time Piper had been home. She had a bit of colour in her cheeks and Piper thought she might have even put on a bit of weight.

'I told you on the phone,' Piper said. 'I didn't come to see you: I'm having dinner with Rob.'

Connie rolled her eyes as if she didn't believe her. 'Everyone's been making such a fuss. Beryl keeps bringing me meals. Lunch and dinner! She says it's no trouble, she just makes a bit extra when she's cooking for the family, but I don't need so much. I don't have a big appetite! Not like you.'

'That's lovely of her,' Piper said, ignoring the dig. 'Where's Buster?'

'Oh,' Connie said, glancing down as if she expected to see him at her heels. 'I think he's asleep on his bean thing.'

Piper followed Connie into the living room where they both immediately saw Buster on the balcony, the doors closed, his little face practically pressed up against the glass. He wiggled delightedly at the sight of Piper and she opened the door and reached down to stroke him while he peed.

'I didn't realise he was out there,' Connie said. 'I thought he was quiet.'

'So,' Piper said, as Buster wriggled past her and jumped up on the sofa. 'What did the hospital say?'

'Come and have a cup of tea first. I haven't got any trifles, but I've got crackers and cheese. And a bit of ham?'

'I'm fine,' Piper said. 'I'm having dinner at Rob's in a bit. But I'll have a tea. Sit down, I'll make it.'

'I'm not an invalid,' Connie said. 'The hospital said I had a thing. I can't remember. Initials. A mini stroke. But nothing to worry about. They've got me on blood thinners. And I'm supposed to cut back on salt.'

'Right,' Piper said. 'And how do you feel?' She actually wanted to ask if she'd been scared. If she was planning to cut back on salt. If she thought there was any way she could maybe not die for a while because Piper really wasn't ready to lose someone else.

'Your sister sent me flowers,' Connie said. 'And chocolates. I gave the flowers to Beryl and the chocolates to Jim. Don't tell them if they come round.'

'That's nice,' Piper said. She'd actually suggested Holly come home with her this weekend, but had received a firm no.

'I can't remember the last time I saw her,' Connie said. 'I don't think I'd recognise her in the street.'

While Connie made the tea, Piper scanned the kitchen for signs that her aunt really wasn't okay, but everything looked the same as always: clean and tidy, tea towels folded neatly on top of the microwave, dishes on the drainer, mugs hanging on hooks under the cupboard.

'Do you have to go back to the hospital?' Piper asked.

'No. I have to see my GP. But I don't know if I'll go. I don't like her. I don't like having a woman GP. Unless it's for lady business.'

Piper tried not to laugh at 'lady business' but failed.

'Oh I know,' Connie said. 'I'm very old-fashioned.'

*

Piper Power Posed until she heard Rob's footsteps at the other side of the door. By the time he opened it, smiling at her in jeans and a long-sleeved black jumper, she was standing like a normal person. A normal person who thought she might be sick from nerves.

'Present for you,' she said, holding out the CD.

Rob took it and stepped back from the door, ushering her inside and following her through to the lounge. The curtains were pulled right back, showing off the amazing river view and a cloudless blue sky. One of the doors was open and the flat felt cool and fresh.

'This looks great,' Rob said, turning the CD over and reading the track listing.

'Yeah, they're good. Everyone at work's pretty excited about their new album. They're recording it at the moment.'

Rob's laptop was standing open on the breakfast bar and he pushed the CD into it, turning the sound up a little.

'Wine?' he asked Piper.

'Please.'

He poured her a glass and Piper cradled it with both hands, leaning back against one of the units.

'How's things?' Rob asked.

'Good,' she said. 'Partly thanks to you actually.'

'Me?'

She nodded. 'Turns out brands are quite keen on bloggers whose photos go viral. And I had two in quick succession. Yours and then one on my Instagram. I mean, the Insta one wasn't quite as big as yours, but then I didn't have your face photoshopped onto my boobs in the Insta one.'

'God,' Rob said. 'I'm so—'

Piper shook her head. 'I know. It's fine, I've told you. You honestly don't have to keep apologising.'

'I want to though.' He grinned.

'You're making me dinner,' Piper said. 'After that we're even, okay?'

'Blimey,' Rob said. 'Better step up my game then.' He held a bowl out towards her. 'Tortilla chip?'

She laughed, taking a couple. 'Wow, quite the host. Didn't get this treatment when I used to go round your house to watch you and Dave watch *Star Wars*.'

'Fuck. We seriously watched it every day for about a year. I can recite it from start to finish.'

'I don't think I ever saw it all the way through. Always fell asleep. Do you keep in touch with Dave?' He hadn't gone to their school – Rob knew him through their mums – so he hadn't been at the reunion.

'Sort of.' He leaned over and switched the oven on at the wall. 'On Facebook. He does a *Star Wars* podcast now. It's massive. He goes to Comic Con and he's interviewed some of the actors.'

'Wow,' Piper said. 'Living the dream.'

'Right? Must admit, I was pretty jealous when he met Mark Hamill. Oh, and he goes out with Claire. You know Claire.'

'Claire Ellis?'

'That's the one.'

'Wow,' Piper said again. 'Never would have put those two together.' Mostly because for years she'd assumed Claire was with Rob.

'How long have they been together?' she asked.

He put an onion on the chopping board and took a knife down from the magnetic strip on the wall.

'Not sure actually. A while.'

'And how long were you together?' Piper asked.

'Who?' He'd peeled the onion and was already chopping it, his hand moving swiftly across the wooden board.

'You and Claire.'

He glanced up at her but didn't stop chopping.

'Careful!' she said instantly.

'I'm fine,' he said, smiling. 'I'm good at this.'

'I know you are. Did you do a course or something?'

He pushed the chopped onion to one corner of the chopping board and started on a piece of celery.

'I've done a few actually. Mum got me one for a present when I moved out of home. It was meant to be sort of a piss-take – you know, like "Rob can't boil water, he'll starve living on his own" kind of thing – but I loved it. So then I did a few more. I've done soups and stews. Indian. Bread and pizza. I love it.'

'Bloody hell. That's very impressive.'

He smiled at her again. 'You haven't tasted it yet. And we were never together.'

He opened the fridge and took out two steaks, sliding them into the pan he was heating on the hob. They sizzled and immediately smelled delicious.

'What?' Piper said.

He was back at the chopping board, halving new potatoes.

'Me and Claire. We were never together. Only ever friends.'

Piper stared at him. 'What?' Why couldn't she form a sentence?

'Do you need more wine?' Rob asked.

'No,' she said. 'Thanks. I'm good.' But it reminded her that she did indeed have wine, and she slugged some.

'We never went out. I never liked her like that. I mean, I didn't like her much at all, a lot of the time. She could be a real bitch. And she was awful to you.'

'But…' Piper said. 'She told me the two of you…'

But even as she was saying it, she wasn't sure if it was actually true. Had Claire told her she and Rob were together? Or had Piper just assumed because she'd seen them together? She wasn't sure.

'She told you that?' Rob said.

Piper finished her wine and reached for the bottle. 'Do you know, I'm not actually sure now. It's so long ago. I guess it doesn't matter.'

'She asked me. More than once. But…' He scraped the onions and celery into a pan and Piper's stomach rumbled immediately.

'But…?' she couldn't help saying.

He leaned back against the worktop and smiled at her. The sleeves of his jumper were pushed up to the elbows. He'd thrown a tea towel over his shoulder earlier, but seemed to have forgotten it was there since he kept picking up another tea towel to wipe his hands on. He looked really good. And he was looking at her like...

'What?' Piper said.

'I was fucking crazy about you,' he said.

'What?' Piper said again. Honestly, she was going to have to do something about this brilliant repartee business – she was barely able to string a sentence together.

'Yeah.' He smiled, shrugged and reached for some plastic tongs to lift the steaks out onto the plates he'd set out earlier.

Piper had no idea what she was supposed to say. Was he making it up? Had he had a head injury at some point in the past ten years that had given him false memory syndrome or something? There was no way he'd been crazy about her back then. It just wasn't possible.

'What about you?' he asked, not looking at her. 'How long have you and Matt been...'

'Me and Matt?' Piper said, genuinely astonished. 'We're not together. God. No. No. Never been together. Well, there was one time... but that was years ago and—' Why was she still talking? She put a thumb up to her lips to shut herself up and then mumbled, 'We're flat-mates. That's all.'

Rob stopped what he was doing and looked at her sideways. 'Yeah?'

'Yeah.'

'Right,' he said. 'Sorry.'

He emptied the new potatoes onto the plate, along with some peas and then carried the plates over to the table.

Piper followed him, still cradling her wine. She couldn't believe he'd said he'd liked her back then. Did that mean he liked her now? Or that he definitely didn't like her now? Matt would say that of course he did: men didn't cook for women they didn't

like. But that didn't mean he like liked her. Just because he had
then – if indeed he had – didn't mean he did now. And he'd
thought she was with Matt. So if he thought she was with Matt
then this had definitely been intended as a friend dinner. Not a
date. Definitely not a date.

Piper sat down opposite him and looked at her plate. Her
stomach was churning so much, she wasn't sure she'd be able to
eat, but it smelled so good.

'This looks amazing,' she said.

Rob noticed the tea towel over his shoulder and slid it off,
draping it over the back of the chair next to him.

'It's easy,' he said. 'But it's a crowd-pleaser.'

Piper cut into the steak and popped a piece into her mouth.
It was good: flavoursome and tender.

'This is really good,' she said, stabbing a piece of potato.

'Do you cook?' he asked.

She shrugged. 'Not really. I assemble, mostly. Usually by the
time I'm home from work I can't be bothered to cook anything
fancy. So I tend to have something bigger – and healthy – at
lunch. There's loads of nice places near work.'

'Your building's on the river, right?'

Piper frowned. 'How did you know that?'

Rob wrinkled his nose. 'Ah. Yeah. I googled.'

Piper laughed. 'Why?'

'You mentioned it one day – you were talking about the girl
band? – and I hadn't heard of it. The company. So I googled it.
And then I'm just kind of nosy about London so I looked it up
on Google Maps and—'

'Wow,' Piper said. 'Stalker.' Maybe it was better that it wasn't
a date. It took the pressure off. She could just relax and be herself
instead of worrying about what might possibly happen after dinner.

'I mean, I couldn't see you on Google Maps…' Rob said,
cutting his own steak.

Piper laughed again. 'One of my colleagues is actually on it. She saw the car going past and so she's captured forever with a what-the-fuck-is-that expression on her face.' Piper ate another piece of steak. Another potato. Drank some more wine. And said, 'I did it too. I looked up this place.' She gestured at Rob's flat. 'And wandered up Vicky Road. Along the prom. Checked to see if the chippy was still there. Looked at our old house. Stopped when I made myself cry. It's a weird compulsion. Like poking a bruise.'

'I get that,' Rob said. 'And maybe it's easier to do it online. You're that bit removed. I can't imagine how painful it must be to actually come back here.'

Piper shook her head. 'Everyone says it gets easier. But I don't know. They're never going to be here.'

'I know,' Rob said. 'I mean… I don't. I'm lucky. But I can imagine. And I understand why you didn't want to come back.'

Piper drank some wine and ate some steak and thought about how so far it had been easier than she'd feared. Coming home. And that Rob was definitely a big part of that.

'You know, you never used to eat,' Rob said, gesturing at Piper's plate.

'What? When?'

'When we were growing up. We'd all go out and get chips or go to McDonald's or whatever and you came too, but you didn't eat. I remember. I noticed once and then I used to look out for it. I think I saw you eat a chip once. But that's it.'

Piper put her cutlery down and stared at him.

'Sorry,' Rob said. 'I shouldn't have—'

'No,' Piper said. 'I'd just forgotten I used to do that. Fuck.'

'Yeah?'

'When you're…' Piper started to say before realising that she was about to say 'when you're fat'. To Rob. Teenage Piper would have died before she referenced her body in front of him, but fuck that. 'When you're fat,' she said, pausing to drink some more wine, 'eating in public is a bit of a headfuck. People comment. And if they don't comment, you can often see them judging anyway. Like on Instagram a photo of a thin girl eating a burger gets comments about how hot it is to see a girl eating, right? Or eating "properly", not a salad, all that shite. But a fat girl eating a burger? You can imagine the comments.'

Rob winced. 'I can.'

Piper laughed. 'Yeah. You definitely got an up-front introduction to being fat online.'

'It's so fucking obnoxious,' he said, topping up her wine. 'And I'm ashamed to say I really wasn't aware of it before I posted that photo. I mean, I knew people were dicks online. And I knew people were particularly dicks to women online, but I'd never seen anything like that. That and the article. The Naomi Jones one.'

'Oh god, yeah. That's a particularly insidious thing. Because it's abuse dressed up as care. How can anyone be offended by "I'm just worried about your health", right? But it's bullshit. There are plenty of unhealthy thin people. People risk their health in loads of different ways every single day and it's no one else's business.'

'Remember when my mum and dad split up?' Rob said. He'd stopped eating and was leaning both arms on the table, his body tilted towards Piper. 'I started self-harming. Just a bit. No one knew. I never told anyone. I used to hit myself, bash my arm against the end of my bed. I didn't think of it as self-harm at the time, I just thought I was getting my anger out, I guess. But that's what it was. And no one knew. No one could have known.'

'I'm sorry,' Piper said. She felt tears building behind her eyes. She'd known him then. She'd hung out with him then. She'd had no idea. He'd seemed fine.

'I'm fine now,' he said. 'And Mum and Dad are fine. They were much happier once they split. But…' He shook his head. 'I don't know why I told you that. I know it's not the same.'

'No,' Piper said. She wanted to reach out and touch him – she sat on her hands instead. 'Thank you for telling me. I wish I'd known back then.'

'Ah,' Rob said. 'No way would I have told you back then. I didn't want you feeling sorry for me. I wanted you to fancy me.'

Piper wriggled her hands out from under her thighs and picked up her wine. 'I did,' she said, before taking a large mouthful.

'You did what?'

'Fucking hell,' Piper said. She couldn't look at him. He was too close. And too hot and she might have had too much wine. 'I did fancy you.'

'You did not.'

She could hear the laugh in his voice. She looked at him. He looked incredulous, smile wide, eyes crinkling at the corners.

'I was completely fucking batshit about you,' she said. 'From the day we met until the day I left.'

She'd definitely had too much wine. Fuck.

Rob was quiet. Staring at her. She forced herself to stare back. She'd never have been brave enough to do this back when they were teens, but she could maybe be brave enough now. Maybe.

'When I walked into the reunion and I saw you…' Rob said. 'I couldn't even approach you straight away. I couldn't catch my breath. You looked… You looked so fucking gorgeous. And then later, when we were dancing, the light was shining on your dress – you were like a glitter ball.' He stopped and shook his head. 'Wait. I don't mean—'

'I know,' Piper said, laughing, even though she was struggling to breathe too. He thought she was gorgeous. He'd really just said that. 'It's okay.'

'Bright and shining and sparkling and…' He drained his wine. 'I'd always thought I was a dickhead for letting you just go off to London. For not telling you or asking you… I almost messaged you so many times. But then I thought, well, you left for a reason.

You didn't keep in touch for a reason. And I didn't want to make you feel like you had to keep in touch or anything. Until I saw you on that show and I just thought "fuck it".'

Piper stared at him. Fuck it. She stood and walked around the table towards him. He turned in his chair, but didn't stand. He looked up at her, and his eyes were dark and focussed on her face.

She grazed his jaw with her fingertips, brushed her thumb along his cheekbone. He spread his legs and she stepped into the V made by his thighs. He reached for her hand, intertwining his fingers with hers. He reached up with his other hand and Piper gasped as he grazed his thumb over her bottom lip. She wanted to kiss him, but at the same time she wanted to stretch the anticipation out forever.

Rob shifted in his seat, his thighs tightening either side of Piper's legs, and she couldn't wait any longer. She dipped her head and pressed her mouth to his and oh god. One of Rob's arms wrapped around her waist, his hand curved around the back of her neck, and she sagged against him as his tongue slipped over her bottom lip.

'Fuck,' she breathed against his mouth.

He huffed out a laugh. 'I know.'

CHAPTER TWENTY-THREE

She pushed her hand into the back of his hair and slipped her tongue against his, tilting her head for better access. She'd had some good kisses over the years. Andrew had been a great kisser. But nothing like this. This kiss started at her lips and zipped down her spine. She thought her toes were probably curling. She pulled back a little, nipping gently at Rob's mouth.

'So,' Rob said. 'You're telling me that we could have been doing this for like fourteen years.'

'God,' she said, dropping her head back. 'Don't.'

She'd barely got the word out before she felt Rob's lips on her neck, his tongue stroking over the muscle.

'There's a mole here,' he said against her neck. 'I never noticed before.'

Piper ran her hands over his wide shoulders. He was basically twice as wide as he had been in their teens – it was ridiculous. He kissed up her throat and she dipped her head down to meet his mouth. The second kiss was just as good as the first, turning hotter faster.

'Can we…' Rob said, his thumb brushing her lip again. She wanted to bite it. 'Can we move to the sofa or—'

'Yeah,' Piper said, breathlessly. She wanted to lie down. She wanted to press herself up against him and feel his hardness against her softness.

He pushed himself up to standing, but immediately kissed her again, her head tipped back this time.

'God,' he said. 'I can't believe—'

'I know,' Piper said.

'Do you want more wine?' Rob asked.

'No,' Piper said. 'Yes.'

'Sit down,' he said. 'I'll open another bottle.'

Piper sat on the sofa, leaning her head against the back and looking up at the ceiling. Her fantasies had featured Rob for years. From the first time they'd met until she'd moved to London. Once she'd left, she'd tried not to think about him any more, but occasionally he'd still crept in. She'd imagined him turning up in London, telling her he missed her, was lost without her, couldn't believe he'd let her get away. In those fantasies she was thin. He'd be stunned. Would gaze at her and say, 'You look amazing.' In those fantasies, she spent as much time thinking about what she was wearing as she did about Rob.

Rob came back with two glasses of wine and set them down on the coffee table, along with the bottle.

'This isn't why I invited you for dinner,' he said, sitting next to her. 'I mean, I'd be lying if I said it didn't cross my mind.' He grinned.

Piper laughed. His thigh was pressed up against hers. She remembered sitting next to him on the bus once, years ago. Claire had sat on his other side, yelling, 'Budge up,' and he'd budged right up against Piper, his body pressed up all along her side. She'd barely breathed for the entire journey, trying to memorise the way he felt.

'I thought maybe it was at first,' Piper said. 'And then when you asked about Matt I thought it couldn't be.'

'I didn't think you were together,' Rob said, dipping his head to graze his lips against her neck again. 'But I needed to make sure first.'

'First,' Piper said.

'First,' Rob confirmed.

Piper turned her head, her lips drifting across his face before finding his mouth. He tasted of wine and steak and pepper. He shifted on the sofa, pressing closer to her, and she relaxed back into the cushions. His hand gripped her hip, fingers pressing into her skin and she arched up into him, moaning into his mouth.

*

Half an hour later, their glasses were empty and Piper was on her back with Rob on top of her, her shirt pushed up to her shoulders, his fingers making patterns against her ribs. She hadn't kissed like this – just kissed – for years. Kissing always seemed to be the starter, gulped down before moving on to the main sex course. And she'd always been okay with that. But then kissing had never been like this. She never wanted to stop kissing Rob. Loved the sounds he made when she bit at his bottom lip or curled her tongue around his. Loved the taste of him and the scent of his neck. Loved how his hips pressed her down into the sofa, how his thigh rubbed against her crotch. Okay, maybe kissing wasn't quite enough.

'Do you want to—' Rob said, pulling himself up and looking down at her.

She ran her hand over the ridiculous muscles in his arm.

'Yeah,' she said.

'Stop?'

'Stop?' She blinked at him. 'Fuck, no.'

Rob laughed. 'Oh. Okay. Good. I thought maybe I was going too fast.'

Piper laughed then. 'It's been fourteen years. Take your clothes off.'

Grinning, Rob pushed himself up to kneeling and pulled his T-shirt over his head.

'Holy shit,' Piper breathed. She'd been touching him, had touched every bit of him over his shirt and under it, but she still hadn't been prepared for how he looked. His chest was wide and muscled, with a patch of fine hair between his nipples. He had an actual six pack, and those ridiculous side grooves, like an Action Man.

'You are ridiculous,' Piper said, before she could think better of it.

Rob grinned at her. 'All these years, when I've thought about you... and me... I dreamed that one day I'd take my clothes off and you'd call me ridiculous.'

Piper laughed. 'I'm sorry.' She shuffled back against a cushion. 'I just keep super-imposing how you used to look over how you look now and it's... a lot.'

'Back atcha.' Rob leaned down to brush his lips over her chest. 'I mean, you were gorgeous then, but now...' He growled into the junction between her shoulder and neck and she laughed as he lowered himself on top of her.

'Actually,' he said, lifting up again. 'I don't know why I'm the only one with my top off.'

Piper sat up just enough to let Rob get hold of the hem of her top and lift it over her head. She closed her eyes until it was off and when she opened them, he was staring down at her with an expression she could only describe as awe.

'You are so fucking gorgeous,' he said.

'It's the bra.'

'It's a good bra,' Rob said. He leaned on his left arm and ran his fingertips from her shoulder, across her chest, along the edge of the bra to the dip between her breasts.

Piper shivered. 'Careful. I saw on the Internet there's a little man living in there.'

Rob laughed. 'God.' He dipped his head and kissed her. 'I really am sorry—'

'Shut up,' Piper said. 'And carry on.'

He ran his finger across the other breast to her shoulder, before curling his hand around the back of her neck, his thumb brushing behind her ear, lowering his mouth to hers again, sucking gently on her bottom lip.

'You're good at this,' she murmured against his mouth.

'I've been thinking about it for a long time.' He dipped his head again, running his tongue along the path made by his finger.

Piper curled against him. 'God. I still can't believe you liked me back then.'

'Same.' He moved lower, kissing her belly, hands sliding over her waist.

Piper tried to move her leg to hook it around his hips, but he was on top of her, pressing her down into the sofa.

'Can we move?' Piper said. 'I'm a bit…'

'Fuck. Am I squashing you? Sorry.'

Rob shifted his leg so it fell to the side of Piper's, their hips aligning, crotches pressing together. Piper tipped her head back. She wanted to move against him, make him move against her, hold his hips and press him tighter into her.

Rob dropped down again, moaning against her neck.

'Can we—Do you want to—'

Piper kissed his neck, the hollow behind his ear. 'Yes.'

CHAPTER TWENTY-FOUR

When Piper woke up she had no idea where she was. The room was pitch dark and totally silent and she blinked up at the ceiling for a second before remembering: Rob. She was at Rob's flat. In Rob's bedroom. In Rob's bed. She rolled onto her side, expecting to find him there, fast asleep, but the other side of the bed was empty, the duvet flapped open like a book.

She reached for her phone and squinted at the brightness. Four a.m. Maybe he'd just gone to the loo. Or maybe she'd been snoring or – god – farting, and he'd gone to sleep on the sofa or in the spare room, if he even had a spare room. She swung her legs out of the bed and tiptoed through to the living room, but there was no sign of him.

The only light in the room was coming from the cooker hood. 'Rob?' she whispered. She didn't like the way her voice sounded in the empty flat. Her stomach started to flutter with nerves. Where the fuck could he be? At four in the morning?

She pulled the curtain back a little and looked out onto the prom. There was no one around, of course. Apart from the water on the river and the occasional seagull, everything was still. Should she phone him? It made no sense that he wasn't here. Maybe there'd been an emergency and he'd had to go, but wouldn't he have left a note?

Pulling the curtain closed again, she checked the bathroom and then the en suite, but both were dark and empty. By the time she climbed back into bed, she was trembling, both with cold and with fear.

She wasn't sure how long she'd been lying there when she heard the front door and then the sound of the shower in the other bathroom.

Why the fuck was he showering? She sat up in bed, leaning back against the pillows. Rob's pillows. She reached for her phone again. It was five now. And Rob was showering. He couldn't have sneaked out to see someone else, surely. That would be mad. But where else could he have gone and why would he need to shower at five a.m.?

Only a couple of minutes later, Rob opened the bedroom door and startled at the sight of Piper, sitting up and staring back at him.

'Shit.' He was naked apart from a towel around his waist. 'Why are you up?'

'Where have you been?' Piper said. She'd hoped to hide the panic in her voice, but knew instantly that she'd failed entirely.

'God, sorry,' he said, coming to sit on the bed next to her. 'I didn't think you'd wake up. I've been for a run.'

'At four in the morning?!'

'Yeah. I don't sleep all that well. I get to sleep, but then I wake up and my mind starts racing and that's it for me. So I started getting up to run and when I get back I can usually get another hour or two of sleep. I would've told you, but I didn't think you'd wake up.'

Piper shook her head. 'I freaked out a bit.'

'Fuck,' Rob said. 'I'm sorry.' He clasped her ankle under the duvet.

'No, it's okay, it's not your fault. I just don't do very well with people...' She swallowed and her throat burned with it. 'Disappearing.'

'Shit,' Rob said, crawling up the bed and sliding an arm around her. 'That's... Yeah, I'm sorry. I didn't even think about it.' He kissed her temple. 'Are you okay?'

Piper nodded. 'Better now you're back, yeah.'

*

'Did you undress me?' Piper asked. 'The night of the reunion?'

They were still in Rob's bed. Neither of them had gone back to sleep. Instead they'd kissed and talked and fucked, and Piper felt boneless, more relaxed than she'd been for as long as she could remember, aching in the best way.

Rob laughed and Piper turned her head, where it was resting on his chest, to look up at him.

'What?'

'No,' he said. 'I wanted to tell you that morning – I didn't want you thinking I'd done it, but I didn't want you worrying about it either. You said you were shame-spiralling.'

'Oh god.'

'Yeah. We got back and you said there was something on the neck that was scratching you. A label, I think? And so you took it off.'

Piper turned her head again, pressing her forehead into his shoulder. 'Oh my god.'

'Didn't even make it to the bedroom. Right there in the lounge.'

'Oh god!' Piper said again.

Rob squeezed her, his arm around her back.

'I couldn't believe my luck. I mean, I knew nothing was going to happen, cos you were…' He sang the next word. 'Hammered! But you stood in the middle of the room, in this amazing under-wear, with your hands on your hips. You said it was—'

'Power Pose,' Piper mumbled into his neck.

He laughed again. 'That's it, I couldn't remember. You sang a bit of the Wonder Woman theme too.'

'Oh god, please stop talking. I'm so sorry I asked.'

'Are the words really something about tights?'

'Satin tights,' Piper said. 'Rhymes with "rights".'

'Fucking hell.'

'I know. It's amazing.'

'You were amazing,' Rob said, kissing her head. 'You were so cute. And really fucking hot.'

'Let's never speak of this again,' Piper said.

CHAPTER TWENTY-FIVE

'Oh my god,' Matt said, as soon as Piper walked into the flat the following day. 'You had sex.'

Piper laughed. 'How? How do you do that?' It had been almost impossible for her not to text from the train and tell him, but she'd forced herself to resist: she'd wanted to see his face when she gave him all the info.

'I can always tell,' Matt said. 'You're all loose. And louche.'

'That's your sex tell, not mine,' Piper said.

Whenever Matt was sleeping with someone he got all loose-limbed and sleepy-eyed, and she could barely convince him to leave the flat at all. Usually when Piper slept with someone it made her even more neurotic than usual, wondering if and when it would happen again, if it had been good for them, if it had been good for her or if she'd just convinced herself it had been because she didn't want to admit it hadn't. It was exhausting. But this time it had been good. There was no question. For both of them. And she knew Rob wanted it to happen again – and as soon as possible – because he'd told her. And she knew she wanted it to happen again because they'd spent so long in bed, she'd almost missed her train. And because she'd spent the entire train journey mentally reliving it all to the point where she'd had to sneak off to the loo to get herself off. Again.

'So?' Matt said, pouring her a glass of wine. 'Give me all the filthy details.'

'I need a shower first,' Piper said.

'Actual filth,' Matt said. 'I'm into it.'

*

'Are you going to go home every weekend now?' Matt asked. 'Cos if you are, I might have to find myself a new flat-mate, know what I mean?'

'It's not every weekend,' Piper had said. 'I didn't go home last weekend.'

'I remember when this was your home,' Matt said dramatically. But Piper knew him well enough to know he kind of meant it, was genuinely concerned. She pulled him down onto the bed next to her, swinging one leg over his thigh.

'Stop trying to get me going,' he said, but immediately sagged against her side.

'This is home,' she said. 'New Brighton is home too. It always has been. But when I'm there, home is here with you. You do the same thing!'

'I do, yeah,' he said. Home for Matt was Sheffield. He only ever went home for birthdays, anniversaries, Christmas. 'But I miss you. I miss our Saturday breakfasts.'

'I miss them too,' Piper said. 'What if, on weekends I'm going home, we have Friday night takeaway instead?'

'Cuts a bit into my social life,' he said, dropping back onto the mattress. 'But okay.'

'I just…' Piper said, lying down next to him, on her stomach. 'I'm worried about Connie.'

'Yeah, Connie. That's why you keep fleeing up the country.'

'It is! I mean, not just Connie.' She smiled, pressing her face into the duvet.

'Yeah, you leave me here while you fuck off for a booty call.'

'Not just a booty call. He's cooking too.'

'Cooking and fucking,' Matt said, stretching up the bed. 'No wonder you can't wait to get away.'

'I don't think I could ever live there again. It's getting easier, going back. But I have to make myself not think about it, about them. And avoid places I know will be too painful. I don't know if I could do that if I lived there.'

Matt raised one eyebrow at her.

'And I don't want to anyway. I love it here. I love our flat. I love Stokey. I love you!'

'Good,' Matt said. 'Cos I don't want to sound pathetically co-dependent or anything, but I'd be fucking lost without you.'

'Same,' Piper said.

'So how *was* Connie?'

Piper pulled a face. 'I barely saw her actually. I had a cup of tea and she gave me a bag of stuff. Actually, there's another thing you'll like.'

She grabbed the bag from her bedroom and handed Matt three wooden deer ornaments.

'Oh my god!' Matt immediately set them on the coffee table and reached for his phone. 'These things are mid-century classics. You could probably sell them on eBay. Were they your parents'?'

'Grandparents', I think Connie said. She gave me a packet of Ryvita too, do you want to Instagram that as well?'

'No, you're alright.' Matt leaned back on the sofa while he picked a filter for the photo.

'So what did you do while I was away?' Piper asked, picking up one of the deer and smoothing her hand over its back. She vaguely remembered them being in her gran's house when she was small.

'More like who did I do, am I right?' Matt said.

It was Piper's turn to give Matt the eyebrow.

'Yeah, you're right. I went out with Jodie on Friday night and spent the rest of the weekend watching *The Crown*.'

'Without me?!'

'Well you weren't here, were you? Oh and I did one of those disgusting foot peel things.'

'Thank fuck I missed that,' Piper said.

'It was amazing though. You'll have to try one.'

Piper swung her legs off the sofa and reached for her laptop. She'd decided to write a blog post about what had happened after Rob posted the photo. About online shaming and viral photos. About why people felt the need to comment on the appearance of strangers on the internet. Plus she had a couple more brands to get back to. It was weird to think that something that had been designed to hurt her – that was if the boys who'd edited her photos had even thought of her as a person, which she doubted – had ended up being positive. She should probably find a way to include that in the post too.

CHAPTER TWENTY-SIX

Piper heard them before she saw them. Shouting and laughter and someone singing. This part – the boring part – of the office was usually quiet, apart from Radio 2 on low, but the band was approaching like a wave and Piper could feel the excitement and anticipation in the air.

When they crashed through the double doors into Legal & Finance, they brought a burst of energy that seemed to make the air brighter. They obviously weren't in performance clothes, but their ordinary clothes were exciting enough. Piper immediately regretted choosing to wear her black dungarees. At least she'd thought to wear her Tatty Devine rainbow parakeet necklace and gold glitter boots. But the girls still made her feel dull. They were so young. And loud. And two of them were really thin, but the other was what the tabloids would describe as 'curvy'.

John opened the door to his office and ushered them inside. He was already blushing and looking flustered. Keith from Marketing followed the girls through the door, along with Juliette from Press. Piper was last in and closed the door behind her, sitting between John and Juliette with her notebook and pen on the table in front of her.

'We're dead excited to be here,' one of the girls – Piper thought it was Chelsea – said in a strong Liverpool accent. Piper hadn't known any of them were from Liverpool.

'We're excited to have you here,' John said stiffly.

'Have you picked a name?' the girl on Chelsea's left asked. Piper knew she was Mia because she was wearing a necklace with it on.

'No,' Keith said. 'We don't want to choose something you're not happy with. Did you have any more ideas?'

'I did,' the third girl – who must have been Frankie – said. 'What about something like 'Sex Toys'? So, like, Pussycat Dolls? It's ironic.'

Piper felt John twitching next to her.

'I think,' Juliette said, 'we want to go for something that younger fans can identify with. So it can be edgy, but not too… age inappropriate, you know?'

'Resting Bitch Face,' Chelsea said. 'We could be RBF for short.'

'Something like that could definitely work,' Keith said. 'But again, I don't think parents are necessarily going to go for something with "bitch"…'

'I was thinking Cherry Bomb?' Mia said. 'But I don't know if something with bomb…'

'I like that one,' Juliette said. 'But maybe some sort of pun…' She closed her eyes and then opened them again. 'I can't think of one.'

'Maybe a flower?' Frankie said. 'The Daisies? Or The Lilies?'

'Oh!' Piper said, sitting up straighter in her seat. 'I saw an article the other day about…' She grabbed her phone and started typing into Google. 'Sorry. It was about flowers that look like vaginas. Or vulvas.'

John coughed.

'Oh wow!' Chelsea said. 'Like that painter! I've seen those paintings online.'

'Georgia O'Keeffe,' Juliette said. 'Lilies. Although she claimed that wasn't her intention.'

'Did she?' Piper asked, glancing up from her phone. 'I didn't know that.'

'Bit embarrassing,' Keith said. 'To have painted all those vaginas accidentally.'

'Found it!' Piper said, tapping on the article. 'Five Flowers That Look Like Vaginas.'

'Is that a real article?' John said.

Piper turned her phone to show him and he winced.

'The first one's a cactus that smells like actual shit,' Piper said, 'so we don't want that one. Poppy?' She turned the phone to show the girls. The photo showed the poppy just coming out of bud and it definitely resembled genitalia.

'I like that,' Chelsea said, leaning forward.

'We know,' Mia said, and all three girls laughed.

'Funny,' Chelsea said. 'No, I mean I like that it looks like a vulva. And that there's, like, hair on it.'

'Is there more photos?' Mia asked.

Piper googled and showed them some more.

'Looks a bit like a scrotum,' Frankie said, pointing at one of them. 'But then the actual flower…'

'I like it,' Mia agreed with Chelsea. 'And Poppy's a good name, right? Like… pop music?'

'And we're, like, pop with an edge,' Frankie said. 'So it could be sort of ironic, right?'

'There's an American singer called Poppy,' Juliette said, looking up from her own phone. 'The Poppies? Does that work?'

'I like it,' Chelsea said.

'There was a sixties girl band called The Poppies,' Juliette said, still looking at her screen.

The girls groaned with frustration.

'What about just Poppies?' John said.

'That's taken too,' Juliette said. She put her phone down on the table. 'Damn. I thought we had it there.'

*

The meeting lasted for much of the afternoon and they still hadn't managed to come up with a name everyone was happy with. They'd dealt with some other issues, though, plus they'd all been thoroughly charmed by the girls. After walking them out, Juliette and Piper had both gone to the loo and, after peeing, standing washing their hands and looking in the mirror, Juliette said, 'You were really good in there. They liked you, I could tell.'

'Thanks,' Piper said. 'I like them. I think they could be really great.'

'Me too.' Juliette shook her hands then reached for a paper towel and folded it in half and then half again. 'I saw this on a TED Talk – shake your hands twelve times then fold one paper towel in half and half again and you only need to use one. Massive effect on the environment if everyone did it.'

'I haven't seen that one,' Piper said, shaking her own hands. 'But I love the Power Pose one. Have you seen it?'

Juliette threw her paper towel in the bin and immediately put her hands on her hips, sticking her chest out and her chin up.

'I love that one! I did it before the meeting.'

Piper laughed. 'Me too.'

'Have you ever considered working in Press?' Juliette asked as they left the bathroom. 'I think you'd be great.'

'I… wow,' Piper said. 'I hadn't. But I will. Thank you.'

CHAPTER TWENTY-SEVEN

When Piper got home from work, she found Holly sitting on the doorstep. Piper's first thought was that Connie had died and Holly had come to tell her in person, but before Piper even got close enough to ask, Holly stood up and said, 'It's okay. No one's died.'

Piper appreciated the fact that her sister understood. But then of course she did, she'd gone through exactly the same thing. Although she hadn't run away to London, she'd stayed behind and lived with Connie for a year after their parents' death.

'What's happened?' Piper said, as she opened the door and her sister followed her inside.

'James has left me,' Holly said blankly.

'What?'

'Yeah. He met someone else. They've been together for over a year, apparently. They're very happy.'

Piper was absolutely gobsmacked. Holly and James had always seemed like the perfect couple.

'Do you know her?' she asked. She couldn't think of what the natural next question should have been.

'A little bit. I've been introduced to her at parties, that kind of thing. And I think she goes to the same gym. But I haven't been going to the gym. Obviously.' She pulled at the front of her size ten top. It was still baggy. Piper tried really hard not to react, but she obviously failed.

'God, I know,' Holly said. 'But I'm not like you! I care what people think about me.'

'Wow,' Piper said. 'Ouch.'

She wasn't even really surprised - Holly had been making similar comments their entire lives – but she was kind of surprised that she was doing it now.

'I'm sorry,' Holly said. 'I didn't mean it like that. You always take it the wrong way.'

'How should I take it?' Piper said, incredulous.

'I meant it as a compliment! Like... you give no fucks. In a good way. Everything I do, I do for someone else's approval. Always have.'

'Wait,' Piper said. 'This is... a lot. First of all: are you okay?'

'Um. No. I'm definitely not okay. But I think... not because of James. I don't think I love him. I'm not sure if I ever actually loved him.'

'Oh what the fuck?!' Piper said. 'Seriously?' She wanted to cry.

'Yeah. I know. I thought I did, obviously. Or I told myself I did. I definitely wanted to. He was perfect. And he was nice to me. And he was rich, that didn't hurt. But I never felt... a spark. We were comfortable. I was comfortable. But it always felt a bit like a business arrangement. I'd read about other couples and how they made each other laugh and were each other's best friend, all that stuff, and wow, could not relate.'

Piper shook her head. 'I thought you were mad about each other.'

Holly smiled tightly. 'No. We were good together. I'm not saying we never had fun. But we haven't had fun for a while. When he told me about her – she's called Rachel – he said he thought we were fine and that he was happy with me until he met her and they started... whatever, that's when he realised that's how it should be. And that we'd never had it at all.'

'Holy fuck,' Piper said. 'I'm so sorry.'

'No.' Holly shook her head. 'It's good, I think? It's for the best. Maybe. Or it will be at some point. I mean, that's not okay, right?

I should want what he has now. I probably should have wanted it all along. I don't know why I didn't.'

Piper stared at her sister for a few seconds. She'd wondered, over the years, if she really knew her, if they really knew each other. It had bothered her that they weren't close, had never really been close – she had friends whose sisters were their BFFs, who talked about how they couldn't manage without them, how lucky they were to have them. After their parents had died, Piper had wondered if they might get closer, but they'd actually become even more distant and she hadn't had any idea how to stop it, wasn't even sure if she wanted to.

'You know what we should do?' Piper said now.

Holly looked up at her. She looked tired. But also hopeful.

'We should go and get absolutely hammered.'

*

Piper rubbed her sister's back as she vomited down the grid.

'Oh fuck,' Holly kept muttering. 'Oh fuck.'

Piper swayed on the edge of the kerb, one hand on Holly's back, the other holding her hair in a ponytail, but pieces kept escaping – it wasn't long enough.

From the coffee shop, they'd gone to a tapas place and quickly moved from Coronas to Margaritas. It had been dark and noisy and Holly had talked about James and work and her house and her friends and while Piper hadn't caught all of it, every bit she had heard had been miserable. Apparently, her sister had been deeply unhappy for a long time and Piper had had no idea.

'I fucking hate throwing up,' Holly said now, straightening up and wiping her mouth with the back of her hand.

'I don't think anyone likes it,' Piper said.

Holly hooked her arm through Piper's. 'How far to your house?'

From the tapas place, they'd crossed the road to a cocktail bar Holly had said she'd read about in *Time Out*. It was dark and sort of sexy and Piper immediately imagined herself there with Rob, perched on one of the leather-topped barstools, Rob standing between her legs, his hands on her hips, giving her that cocky smile of his that made her want to bite him on the neck like a vampire.

They'd tried a couple of different cocktails – which Piper had known was a mistake, but Holly had been very determined – and had ended up with something called a Perfect Storm, which seemed appropriate.

'My fucking life,' Holly had said, holding up the glass.

'What are you going to do?' Piper had asked.

'Fuck everything and start again,' her sister had said. 'Like you did.'

Piper helped her down the steps to her flat. She put the key in the door and Holly leaned heavily against her.

'I really don't recommend that,' Piper said.

'Have you got wine?'

'You can't drink wine now,' Piper said, pushing the door open. It scraped against the tiles. 'You need to go to sleep.'

'I've been sick,' Holly said. 'I feel fine now.'

'No,' Piper said. 'No way. I'm going to get you some water.'

Holly followed Piper down the hall, past Piper's bedroom and into the lounge. She slumped down on the sofa and reached down to tug off her shoes. Piper got them both glasses of water and sat down on the sofa next to her, the water on the coffee table.

'Drink some,' Piper said. She felt more sober than she should have, considering what she'd drunk too. But she'd been drinking tap water as well. And she'd eaten before they'd met up – no doubt Holly hadn't.

'Are you hungry?' Piper asked her sister. 'Do you want some toast?'

'What time is it?'

Piper glanced up at the Flap clock Matt had bought her as a housewarming present. 'It's only ten.'

'Ugh,' Holly said. 'It feels later. Maybe one piece of toast. No butter.'

'Oh fuck off,' Piper said, getting up again and taking her own glass of water with her into the kitchen. 'Peanut butter? Jam? Both?'

'Oh god,' Holly said. 'Both. I've never tried that.'

'Jesus. You haven't lived.'

'I haven't! That's what I've been saying.' When she bit into the toast, she moaned and closed her eyes. 'This is really good. It sounds gross. But it's good!' She opened her eyes, stared at Piper.

'I know.'

'Can I ask you something?' she said, spraying crumbs.

'Of course.'

'So you just… eat whatever you want?'

'God,' Piper said, picking up her own piece of toast. 'Yes. Pretty much.'

'How?'

'How?' Piper frowned. 'I just… I like food. I spent a long time trying to diet or "cut down" or "be good" or whatever and it's all just bullshit. It's just food. It's not good or bad. Some of it is better for you, obviously, but there shouldn't be any morality attached to it. Like, not having a piece of cake isn't virtuous – it doesn't make you a better person. If you're hungry, you eat, that's it.'

'I was shitty to you when we were younger,' Holly said.

Piper didn't mention that she was still shitty to her pretty often. 'Yeah,' she said instead. 'You were.'

'It was just… everything seemed to be so easy for you, you know?'

Piper let out a bark of laughter before she could stop herself. 'Are you serious?'

'You were Mum and Dad's favourite. Both of them. You did really well at school. You had these amazing friends. And I just felt like I was trying so hard all the time but never quite getting it right. And I never knew why.'

Piper shook her head. 'I never knew you felt like that. I never had any idea.'

Holly smiled. 'I used to want to ask you how you did it. But I didn't want you to know I was faking fucking everything.'

'I always felt I was faking everything too,' Piper said. 'But not even well. Like everyone knew I was faking badly.'

'No,' Holly said. Her eyes were starting to close. 'No way.'

'And I always thought you were Dad's favourite,' Piper said. 'He talked about you all the time. He was so proud of you.' Her voice cracked.

'You too,' Holly said. One eye was open, but the other was half closed. 'I miss them so much.'

Piper nodded, swallowing. 'You need to go to bed.'

'I'll sleep here,' Holly said. She reached up and quickly wiped her face. 'It's okay.'

'Give over. You can sleep in my bed with me.'

'Is there room?' Holly said. 'I don't mean because—Oh fucking hell. I just mean, is there room?'

Piper laughed. 'There's room.'

*

'Jesus Christ,' Matt said, as Piper opened the door. 'What happened to you?'

Piper shushed him. 'Holly's here. She's still asleep. We went out last night and it got messy.'

He followed her into the flat. She pulled her bedroom door closed on the way past.

'I'm assuming you were the only one who got messy?' Matt said, as Piper filled the kettle.

She shook her head. 'Nope.' She leaned closer to him so she could whisper. 'James has left her. She's quit her job. Everything is fucked up. She told me she was pretending all the time and was jealous of how easy everything was for me.'

'What the actual fuck?'

'I know. And she tried to get me to ring you and invite you over. She's warm for your form.'

'Never say that again. And let me repeat: what the actual fuck?'

'I know.' She took three mugs down from the shelf and dropped in teabags.

'And here I was thinking I was bringing primo goss along with a maple bacon pancake.' He held out a polystyrene box.

'Fucking hell, Matt. You lead with the maple bacon pancake, god!' She flipped the lid and her mouth immediately watered.

'Should I go back and get one for Holly?'

Piper put the box down while she made the tea. 'I doubt she'll be up for a while. She puked outside the undertaker's.'

'Holly? Your sister Holly? Your goody two shoes, practically-perfect-in-every-way sister Holly?'

'Yes. That one. And shush!'

'I'm just struggling to get my head round it. I don't think I've ever even seen her looking slightly dishevelled, never mind puking—'

'In a grid. Outside an undertaker's.'

'Is it wrong that I'm immediately finding her more attractive?'

'Yes. You weirdo.'

They sat down at Piper's small dining table with their teas, two forks, and the bacon pancakes between them. Saturday mornings with Matt were one of the very best parts of Piper's life.

'Did you go out last night?' she asked him. 'You look surprisingly bright-eyed.'

'That's what I was going to tell you. I went out for one. With Rebecca. And finished with her.'

'Oh. Oh wow.'

'Yeah.' He folded a piece of bacon into his mouth.

'How did she take it?'

'She was… not best pleased.'

'Oh no.'

'Apparently she thought I was going to ask her to move in with me.'

'What? Why?'

Matt shrugged. 'I don't actually know. She kept saying it was the next step and I was like… we're really not there yet. I mean, even if I was happy with her I think it'd be too soon to move in, right?'

'I think so? But I don't know that there are actual timescales.'

'Oh apparently there are. She said there are. And we were at the very least approaching moving in time. So.'

'Did she cry?'

'She cried. She yelled. She threw a drink at me.'

'Oh god.'

'And some crisps.'

Piper covered her mouth as she laughed. 'Where was this?'

'The Queens.'

'Oh no.'

'People stared.'

'I bet they did.' Piper dragged some pancake through the syrup. 'How do you feel about it? Are you okay?'

'I feel fine, actually. I mean, I feel shitty for upsetting her. But I felt less shitty as soon as she threw the drink at me.'

'And the crisps.'

'And the crisps. I'd been enjoying them too.'

Piper's bedroom door creaked as it opened and Holly appeared. Her hair was matted to her face, and her eyes were still mostly closed. She was wearing a T-shirt Piper had given her and it hung off her thin frame. She saw Matt, squeaked with horror and disappeared back into the bedroom, slamming the door.

*

The next time Holly appeared, she was wearing her own clothes – a drapey black top with sheer sleeves over tight dark jeans. She'd brushed her hair and removed last night's make-up – presumably with the wipes Piper kept on her bedside table. She looked younger and softer than she usually did. Matt looked at Holly then turned back to Piper and widened his eyes.

Piper got up, pushing her chair back. 'Sit down, I'll make you a tea. How do you feel?'

'Not great,' Holly said. She sat down on the sofa and stepped into her boots.

'Sit at the table,' Piper said. 'I'll make you some toast. Sorry, we've eaten all the pancakes.'

'I can go and get more,' Matt said. 'They were really good.'

'What were they?'

'Bacon and maple syrup.'

Holly stared down at the floor and then said, 'That would be great. Please. If you really don't mind.'

'I really don't,' Matt said, standing up. 'I'll be ten minutes.'

'Wow,' Holly said, once Matt had gone. 'You two aren't...?' She waved her hand.

'God,' Piper said. 'No.'

'But you are seeing someone? Is it Robbie?'

'Rob. And yeah. I guess. I mean, I've had dinner with him and... stuff. But we're not, like, together or anything.'

Her sister stared at her for so long that Piper started to freak out.

'You've always been totally yourself,' Holly said. 'I think I've always resented that. And now you're actually going out with the boy you were crazy about as a teen.' She shook her head. 'I need some of whatever you're on.'

'You're fine, Hol. You've always been fine.'

'But I've never really been happy,' Holly said.

Piper was shocked to realise her sister was crying. She hadn't seen her cry since, well, since the funeral.

Holly scrubbed at her face with flat hands. 'I've been thinking I should try to be less... me.' She laughed. 'I should try to be more like you.'

'I don't think—'

'No, I don't mean… I mean, you don't have to worry about me. I just think… all this time I've been trying to be this perfect person and that wasn't me. And I don't even really know who "me" is. And so maybe I should try something different.'

'You could try coming home,' Piper suggested. 'I'm going again next weekend.'

Holly winced. 'I don't think so.'

So maybe she hadn't changed after all.

CHAPTER TWENTY-EIGHT

'This is the worst thing that's ever happened to me,' Piper said, rolling onto her side and curling down further under the duvet. Rob's bed was comfy. And warm. She did not want to get out of it.

'You asked me to wake you up,' Rob said. Piper could hear the amusement in his voice. 'In fact, you begged me.'

'I didn't beg,' Piper said. 'And I must've been drunk. Why would I want to get up and go running in the middle of the fucking night?'

'It's not the middle of the fucking night. It's almost morning. I slept really well. Can't imagine why.'

Piper opened one eye and peered up at him. It was definitely still dark – she could only see the shape of him looming over her. But she could tell he was smiling. She pushed herself up on one arm and kissed him. He tasted of toothpaste.

'Forget about running,' Piper said. 'Come back to bed. I can give you a good workout. Really put you through your paces.'

Rob laughed and straightened up. 'I've already got my trainers on. Are you coming or not?'

'I could be,' Piper said. 'If you weren't making me go out for a run.' But she was already swinging her legs out of bed.

*

Their footsteps echoed on the empty pavement. Piper was only aware of the cold air, her breath, Rob next to her, the still water of the river over the wall. She knew why he liked it. It was like being the first people in the world. The only people in the world. She'd never known the prom so quiet and empty.

'You do this every night?' Piper asked, her breath coming fast. She was running at the same speed as Rob, but his strides were longer so he kept getting slightly ahead and having to jog on the spot until she caught up.

'Not every night,' Rob said. 'Most nights. I don't sleep when I don't.'

'And you've tried running in the day like a normal person?'

Rob laughed. 'Yeah. That's good too. But this is better. Honestly, I've tried everything else, but this is what works.'

'Wow,' Piper said, slowing to a walk. 'I can feel my pulse in my face.'

Rob slowed too, walking alongside her. 'I wouldn't expect you to come with me. I just wanted you to know—'

'Race you to the clown statue,' Piper said, running again.

Rob overtook her easily before turning and running backwards, goading her.

'You're a shit,' she said. 'I don't know why I like you.'

He stopped immediately. 'You like me?'

'You know I like you,' Piper said. 'God.'

Once she was past him, she started to jog again.

'I hoped you liked me,' he said. 'I kind of assumed you did since you keep coming back. But you never said.'

'I mean, do I have to spell out everything?' Piper said. 'Couldn't you just, you know, infer?'

'Hey,' Rob said, grabbing her wrist and stilling her with his other hand on her shoulder. 'Look.'

She turned and gasped at the sight of dozens of rabbits running down over the rocks and the grass that separated the prom from the road behind. Their white tails flashed in the darkness and there were so many of them she couldn't quite catch them all in her mind.

'Is this why you like running at night?' Piper whispered.

Rob hooked his chin over her shoulder, his arms sliding around her waist from behind. 'Part of it, yeah. First time I saw them I shit myself. One darted out in front of me. It was like something from a Stephen King novel or something. I thought I was going to be swarmed.'

'Local night runner savaged by rabbits,' Piper said.

She felt Rob's laughter against her back. 'What a way to go.'

'What are they doing?' Piper said. They seemed to be running every which way, without intent.

'Dunno,' Rob said. 'Maybe they're just out for a night run too?'

'Couldn't sleep,' Piper said.

'Rabbity anxiety dreams.'

Rob unhooked his arms from her waist, but grabbed her hand. They started walking again.

'National carrot shortage,' Piper suggested.

They walked as far as the Pierrot and then Rob said. 'Do you want to go back?'

'Not really,' Piper said. 'This is nice.'

They crossed the road and carried on to the beach. The tide was out and they sat down on a cement bench, looking out at the water.

'I wish we'd done this back then,' Rob said.

Piper smiled. 'I don't know. We probably would've fucked it up if we had. This is better.'

'So you don't think we're going to fuck this up then?'

Piper looked at him. He was leaning back against the bench, long legs stretched out in front, crossed at the ankles. Piper was cold, but Rob didn't seem to be bothered at all – totally relaxed. She shuffled along the bench and leaned against him, and he immediately wrapped one arm around her shoulders, pulling her closer.

Light was just starting to show on the horizon: a thin line of pink.

'Can we stay for the sunrise?' Piper asked. 'Or will it take too long?'

'We can stay,' Rob said. 'We'll probably need to huddle together for warmth though.'

By the time they'd stopped kissing – Rob's warm hands roaming under Piper's hoodie – the sky was almost entirely pink streaked with orange. Piper looked over Rob's shoulders: the rabbits had all gone.

'I think they only come out in the dark,' he said, even though she hadn't mentioned what she was looking for.

'You and the rabbits,' Piper said.

'And now you too,' Rob said, dipping his head to kiss the side of her neck.

'Only this time,' Piper said. 'Never again.'

'Never?'

'Next time you can wake me up when you get back. And I'll warm you up.'

'Deal,' Rob said.

They walked back along the prom, holding hands, and stopped at Starbucks, even though, as Rob said, he had a perfectly good coffee machine at home. But Piper was cold and tired and, if she was honest, kind of wanted to show Rob off. Even if it was only to a barista she didn't even know.

*

In Starbucks, a woman had come rushing up to Piper, saying 'Oh my god!' She'd clutched both of Piper's hands and said, 'It is you, isn't it? Piper?'

It was only then that Piper had realised who it was: Dee, one of her mum's friends.

'Gosh, it's so good to see you,' she'd said. 'You look so much like your mum.'

And Piper had burst into tears.

Dee had been full of apologies and Piper had apologised too, and hugged her, and then she and Rob had left without their coffees. On the way back to his flat, he'd been quiet, squeezing her hand, but not asking her anything or encouraging her to talk and she'd really appreciated it.

Now, on his balcony, she stared out at the water. 'It was always easier to pretend they weren't really gone if I didn't come home,' she said.

Rob nodded, his hand on her knee. She curled her hands around the coffee he'd made for her as soon as they'd got back.

'I don't want to forget them.' Piper swallowed a sob. 'It's just easier when everything doesn't remind me of them, you know? Like I can picture them here in so many places – my mum looking up at the blossoms in the park. My dad waiting in the queue in the chippy. But then there's all this new stuff too. Like the cinema and Wetherspoons and these flats. And I don't have memories of them here. But it seems wrong that they never knew them too. Do you know what I mean?'

'I can understand that it must be bittersweet,' Rob said.

'That's exactly the word.'

*

'When will you be back next?' Rob asked later as she packed her bag, looking around his room for anything she might've missed.

'First weekend of next month, maybe?' Piper said, heading into the bathroom for her toothbrush.

'You know,' Rob said. 'You could leave that here. So you don't need to worry about forgetting it next time.'

'But then how would I clean my teeth in London?' Piper joked, leaning down to kiss him as she dropped her toothbrush into her toiletries bag.

Rob grabbed her hips and steered her between his thighs. 'Leave it all. I'll take care of it until you come back.'

'But what if I don't come back?' Piper said. 'Then I'd be out a shitload of make-up. Do you know what that stuff costs?'

Rob's hands dropped down to his sides. 'I dread to think. I'm just saying. If you wanted to leave anything here, you could.'

'Maybe a toothbrush,' Piper said. 'Next time. I'll buy another when I get home.'

She zipped her bag up. 'Done.'

'I'll take you to the station,' Rob said.

'You don't need to do that,' Piper said, as she always did. Even though she loved it. She loved him walking her to her train, kissing her on the platform, smiling through the window as the train pulled away. He'd got on board once to put her bag on for her and she'd half hoped the train would leave and he'd have to go back to London with her. Even though that wouldn't work. Her life in London was something else entirely. She couldn't imagine how Rob would even fit in there.

CHAPTER TWENTY-NINE

'We read your blog,' Chelsea told Piper.

They were in John's office again, this time with representatives from International and Digital. They really needed to come up with a name because the launch had been booked – on a super-yacht of all things – so the plan was basically that they'd hang out and chat and brainstorm until someone came up with something. (Angus from Digital had already suggested 'Brainstorm', which had then sent them googling for rhymes and briefly considering 'Reign' before the girls almost wet themselves laughing at the idea of being called 'Champagne'. Or 'Cocaine'.) They'd already been there so long they'd eaten a full plate of sandwiches and a packet of Cadbury's Fingers that Mia had brought with her. The girls showed no signs of flagging, but everyone else in the room was starting to droop.

Piper stared back. 'Seriously?'

'Yeah. We looked you up after last time. Cos we loved that vagina thing you found. You know, the flowers?'

Piper nodded. She didn't dare look at John.

'You're really cool,' Frankie said.

Piper laughed. 'I don't know about that.'

'No, you are. Like, the post about the photos going viral? That's such bullshit. That people do that kind of thing, I mean. You looked fierce in both of the photos and people trying to shame you should just fuck off.'

'I downloaded this app,' Chelsea said. 'Whenever anyone sends me a dick pic, it puts a little hat on it – or you can do, like, glasses or googly eyes – and I send it back.'

John was making a gurgling noise. Piper hoped he wasn't actually dying.

'That's brilliant,' she said.

'Right?' Chelsea said. 'I don't think girls – women – should have to put up with it. And it's great that we're going to have this platform to tell them that. Obviously the music's more important, but that's still really valuable too, right?'

'It's just a shame it's needed,' Frankie agreed.

Something was tugging at the edge of Piper's brain. She wanted to shush everyone in the room, but instead she said, 'Does anyone want a coffee? I think I'll do a Starbucks run. I need to stretch my legs.'

While she waited for the coffees, she scrolled through Rob's messages on her phone. He was definitely good at texting, able to take her from laughing to wanting to get on the next train and rip his clothes off in one text. It was when she got back to the text he'd sent her when she was on the train home on Sunday evening that she remembered.

*

'What do you think about "Bitter/Sweet"?' she asked, setting everyone's coffees down on the table.

For a second, the room was so silent Piper could hear the dance music coming up through the floor from the Production department below. And then Chelsea said 'Holy shit. I love it.'

*

The rest of the day was spent confirming the name with anyone who might have any objections, but everyone seemed to love it and Piper was buzzing with the thrill of having come up with the name herself.

'You're going to be working with us, right?' Chelsea had asked Piper as they'd been leaving, just as giddy and exuberant as they'd been when they'd arrived hours earlier.

'Not really,' Piper said. 'Unfortunately. I'm in Legal so once the contract's done my bit's over really.'

'That's a shame,' Chelsea said. 'You should quit and come and work with us.' She hugged Piper – as did the other girls – and then they left, leaving Piper standing in the foyer, feeling oddly disappointed.

Halfway up the stairs her phone buzzed with a notification and she stopped to read it, expecting it to be a text from Rob. But it was from Instagram, to tell her that all three girls had followed her account. Instead of heading up the second staircase to Legal, she turned into the Press department and knocked on Juliette's door.

As she walked in, Juliette looked up from her laptop, her eyes bright. 'Hey, superstar!'

'Hey,' Piper said. 'Were you serious about that job in Press?'

CHAPTER THIRTY

Piper knocked on Matt's door.

'I've got good news and I've got champagne!' She turned the bottle round in her hands. 'Well, it's Prosecco, cos I'm getting a raise, but I haven't got it yet, so—'

'Hang on!' Matt called from inside.

'Can I come in?' Piper asked, resting her forehead on the wood. 'We can drink it in your bed like Kardashians. Probably.'

'I'm, um, not alone,' Matt called.

Piper could hear thumps and rustling. She didn't know why he was being so coy. She'd met Jack. She liked Jack. Jack liked her. She thought. Maybe he didn't? Maybe it wasn't Jack. It was probably Becks. Matt was so fickle.

She stumbled a little as Matt opened the door she'd been leaning on and stepped into the hall, pulling it closed behind him.

'What's the matter?' Piper asked. 'Why are you being weird when I've got good news and Prosecco?' She held up the bottle and waved it at him, grinning.

He was wearing sweatpants and no shirt. He put his hands on her shoulders and steered her towards the kitchen.

'Does Jack not like me?' she said. 'Wait. Have you been doing something kinky? Is he tied up? Have you left him dangling from the ceiling? I'm not sure the beams are—'

'It's not Jack,' Matt said, flicking the kettle on. 'Don't freak out.'

'I'm not going to freak out. Your filthy business is your filthy business. What happened to Jack though? He was cute. Is it Becks?'

'Don't worry about Jack. No, it's not Becks. And don't yell when I tell you.'

'Fucking hell,' Piper said. 'I'm not going to yell.'

'I think you might yell.'

'Matt,' Piper said.

'Piper.' He took her favourite mug down from the shelf.

She stared at him, eyebrows raised.

'It's Holly.'

At first, she genuinely couldn't think what he could mean. And then... 'Holly. My sister Holly.'

'Yes. Your sister Holly.'

'My sister Holly is in your bed. And you've had sex.'

'Yeah. No. I mean, I don't know that you need details of—'

'Holly?' Piper yelled, pushing past Matt and heading for his room.

'You said you weren't going to yell,' Matt said, following her.

Piper pushed the door open. Her sister was sitting at the end of Matt's bed. She was fully dressed, apart from one boot, which she was pulling on. She wasn't wearing any make-up and she had sex hair.

'You've got sex hair,' Piper said.

'Piper,' Holly said, standing up and holding her hands up in front of her. 'It's not what it looks like.'

From behind her, Piper heard Matt laugh. 'I mean, it kind of is.'

'Well. Yeah,' Holly said. 'This is. But we haven't been... behind your back.'

'Apart from today,' Piper said. 'Because Matt sure as shit didn't tell me you were coming over. And neither did you.'

'It wasn't planned,' Holly said. 'I just... I've had a shitty day. And I bumped into Matt. And you know, you knew, that I...' She shook her head. 'You know.'

'Fancied him?' Piper said. 'I think once you've shagged him, it's okay to admit you fancy him.'

'It's not about him,' Holly said. 'I'm just… I'm so fucking miserable. I just needed… something.'

Piper glanced behind her, but Matt wasn't there any more and she was glad.

'I'm sorry you're unhappy,' Piper said. 'But also I don't really give a shit. You don't come to my flat and fuck my best friend behind my back. That's just… that's just not something a person does. So if it's okay with you, I'd appreciate it if you just fucked off.'

'Can we just talk about this,' Matt said. 'I've made you a brew. Sit down and we can talk and—'

'I'm going home,' Piper said. She was still holding the Prosecco. She slammed it down on the table and watched some tea jump out of the mug.

'You're going tomorrow morning, aren't you?' Matt said. 'Why don't I go and get a takeaway and—'

'I don't want a takeaway,' Piper said. 'I'm going to go tonight. So, you know, the flat's all yours. Feel free to carry on fucking my sister.'

'Piper,' Matt said, holding his hands out and stepping towards her. She took a step backwards. 'Just… calm down. I know you're upset, but—'

'Fuck off, Matt.' She pushed past him to get to her room. 'I know you do what you want and you don't give a shit who you do it with, but I always thought you gave a shit about me.'

'Jesus Christ.' Matt stopped in her bedroom doorway. 'You know I do. I know we shouldn't have done this. I know I shouldn't have, but if you'd just—'

Piper pushed her door closed with Matt on the other side and leaned back against it. She heard the front door slam and knew it was Holly leaving. She wanted to lie face down on her bed and cry. Or drink the entire bottle of Prosecco and forget any of this had happened. Instead she shoved some clothes into her weekend bag and yanked her door open again.

'Holly's gone,' Matt said. He was sitting at the dining table, the tea he'd made for Piper cooling in front of him.

'And now I'm going,' Piper said.

'Don't. Stay and talk.'

'I don't want to talk to you,' she said.

And then she left.

CHAPTER THIRTY-ONE

By the time Piper got to Rob's she was calmer. Not calm – she'd cried on the train and typed and deleted a bunch of angry texts to both Holly and Matt, before buying herself a tiny bottle of wine and downing it while staring at her own reflection in the window. She'd also texted Rob to tell him she would be turning up about fifteen hours earlier than expected. He was at his mum's, but said he'd get home in time to meet her.

Now he pushed the door closed behind her and stepped up to her, caging her against the door with his arms. She dropped her bag.

'You smell amazing,' he said, dipping his head to kiss her neck.

'Cheesy,' she muttered, but she was already melting. It was embarrassing how quickly he could make her knees weaken.

'Hmm, I don't think it's cheese,' he said, leaning back to smile at her. 'But whatever it is, I like it.'

She reached up and curled her hands over his biceps, leaning forward to kiss him.

'Hi,' he said, smiling.

'Hi.'

'Have you eaten?' he asked, as she followed him into the flat.

She hadn't, she realised. She'd been too angry to eat. But now she realised she actually was hungry.

'I can make you an omelette?' Rob said, opening the fridge and staring at the contents. 'Or boiled eggs and soldiers.'

'God,' Piper said. 'That sounds really good actually.'

She watched him fill a pan with water and put it on the stove.

'When I was little,' Piper started to say. And then stopped as her throat tightened.

Rob glanced over his shoulder at her. 'Go on.'

'You're hot when you cook,' she said instead, coming up behind him and wrapping her arms around his waist.

'You really shouldn't distract the chef,' Rob said.

Piper kissed the back of his neck, nuzzling her nose into his hair. His stomach muscles tightened under her hands and she pressed closer.

'Let me just—' he said, his voice cracking.

'Why don't we have the eggs after?' she suggested.

She hooked her fingers into the waistband of his jeans and he turned the hob off and let himself be pulled into the bedroom.

*

'I was in Ibiza, on a cycling tour,' Rob said, rolling onto his back.

They'd got up once, eaten boiled eggs and soldiers smothered with butter and then gone back to bed again.

'Are you making this up?' Piper asked. 'It sounds like the "I was walking in the foothills of Mount Tibidabo..." story from *Friends*. Have you started watching it yet, by the way?'

Rob laughed. 'No. And I'm not making it up. A bunch of us went. We had, like, a week's cycling and then a week clubbing.'

'Christ,' Piper said. 'You can't just have a proper holiday? Have to flog yourself first?'

Rob slid a hand down Piper's chest, between her breasts, and then curled it round her waist, dropping his head to kiss her on the shoulder. 'There was no flogging. Anyway. I met this girl.'

'Was she cycling too? Cos I fear for her fanny if she was.'

'No. I met her in the second week. In a bar.'

'Good.'

'And we got on really well. And then we went back to her hotel room. Is this making you jealous? At all?'

It was a bit, but there was no way Piper was going to tell him that. 'No. You're fine. Carry on.'

'And I started going down on her... and I'll never forget what she said.' He brushed his lips over Piper's neck. 'She said, "Oh Christ, what the fuck are you doing?"'

Piper snorted with laughter. 'Seriously?'

'Yep. She actually pushed my head away. She said, "Who the fuck told you that felt good?"'

'God, Rob,' Piper said. 'What were you actually doing?'

'Now it's a while ago and drink had been taken so I'm not sure. But I imagine I was probably just, like, mashing my face in there.'

Piper laughed again, rolling onto her side so she could look at him.

'There may have been some licking? But I think it'd be more like a cow stripping the paint off a car.'

'What?'

'My grandad told us that he parked next to a field once and when he came back the cows had licked the paint off his car.'

Piper stared at him. 'So. Many. Questions.'

Rob tipped his head and pressed his lips to hers. 'Never mind that.'

'Right,' Piper said. 'You've got skills to show me.'

'Silky skills,' Rob said, kissing down the side of her neck.

'Always sport with you.'

He kissed between her breasts, following the path his hand had taken earlier. His hands now were sliding down her sides towards her hips. She sucked in a breath as he nuzzled her belly and kept moving lower. His hands pushed under her bum and she curled her pelvis up to meet his mouth.

'Holy shit,' she murmured, sliding one hand into the back of his hair.

She felt like she was melting into the bed – Rob's hands on her hips, his tongue on the inside of her thighs. Then everything was blackness and static before her orgasm overtook her and white light burst behind her eyes. She felt like she was shattering into pieces, exploding all over the room. Bits of her embedded in the walls and the ceiling forever.

*

'Do you keep in touch with Ibiza girl?' Piper asked after. Both of them were lying on their backs, gazing up at the ceiling, Rob's foot hooked around her ankle.

'Her name was Belle. And no.'

'Her name wasn't fucking Belle,' Piper laughed. 'That's the name she gave you.'

'Her name could've been Belle! You don't know.'

'Belle.' Piper laughed. 'God.'

'Your name's Piper!'

Piper grinned. 'Piper's not a Disney princess. Anyway. I'd like to send made-up-name-Belle a present. Maybe a car. Or a house.'

'Good, right?' Rob said, rolling on his side again and nuzzling against her.

'A whole new world,' Piper said.

'I think I'm falling in love with you,' Rob said, his face pressed against the side of her neck.

Piper pulled back to look at him, her hand curved around his jaw, thumb brushing his bottom lip. 'No.'

He smiled. 'What do you mean "no"?'

'No. That's not... that's not what this is.' She wanted to get out of bed, but Rob's ankle was hooked around hers, his hand resting on her waist.

'What is it then?' Rob asked, his eyebrows pulling together.

'It's...' Piper started. 'It's... fun. It's... you live up here. And I live down there. And neither of us is going to move so it just has to be fun.'

'I'm having fun,' Rob said. 'Why does that mean I can't fall in love with you?'

Piper shook her head, closing her eyes. 'Because!'

'Because…?'

'Because that's just not what's meant to happen.'

Rob dipped his head to kiss Piper gently, her thumb still between their lips. 'Well I wish you'd told me this when we first started. I would have tried really hard not to fall in love with you. But you didn't tell me. So…'

'So nothing,' Piper said.

'So I think I'm falling in love with you.'

Piper dipped her head, hiding her face in the curve of his neck. 'No.'

'I mean, you can say no as much as you like,' Rob said, hand sliding round to the small of her back, pulling her more firmly against him. 'Makes no odds to me.'

'Stop talking about it.' She licked the side of his neck. She loved the way he tasted there, salty and warm.

'I'll stop talking about it now,' Rob said, rolling her onto her back, bracing himself on top of her. 'But I'm going to bring it up again, just so you know.'

Piper shook her head again. It was ridiculous. He was being ridiculous.

'You don't need to say it back, if that's what's bothering you,' Rob said.

'That's not it.' Piper hooked her legs around his thighs. 'You don't need to say it at all.'

'But I want to say it.'

'And I don't want to hear it.'

'What if I whisper it?' Rob said, his mouth moving round to her ear, lips grazing her earlobe.

'No,' she said. She rolled away from him. 'Look, I'm going to go and stay at Connie's.'

He reached for her. 'Don't do that. I'll shut up. I can think of a few ways to keep my mouth busy.'

'It's not that,' Piper lied. 'I just think I should go. I keep coming home and seeing you and barely seeing Connie and—'

'Pipes, it's the middle of the night!'

Piper was standing now, pulling on her clothes from where she'd left them on the floor.

'It's okay, I've got a key. And this way I can see her in the morning. She said she's got something she wants to show me.'

Rob sat up in bed. 'You really don't have to go. You shouldn't walk up there on your own.'

'It's fine,' she said. 'It's Friday night, it'll still be busy.' She knew it was – she could hear music from the pubs through Rob's open bedroom window. 'This was really good. I'll see you tomorrow, yeah?'

'Piper,' Rob said. He was out of bed now too, but he hadn't bothered getting dressed. He followed her through the flat, naked.

At the door she turned and kissed him quickly, one hand flat on his chest to hold him back.

'It's not because of what you said,' she told him.

But she knew neither of them believed her.

CHAPTER THIRTY-TWO

'I didn't know you still had this,' Piper said the next morning, grasping for the handle and then sliding the heavy box out from under the bed.

Connie had still been awake when she'd arrived in the night – even though it had been gone midnight – and she hadn't even seemed surprised to see her. Piper hadn't slept – she'd read the texts Holly and Matt had sent her (Holly's passive aggressive, Matt's pleading) and lain awake, staring at a water stain in the corner of the ceiling and thinking about how quickly a life could fall apart.

'I almost chucked it when I moved,' Connie said, her voice muffled because she was rummaging in the bottom of the wardrobe. 'But I thought you might want it. Or your sister. But I forgot to mention it to you.'

'You've got the slides too, right?' Piper said, her voice scratchy with tiredness and tears. The thought that her aunt might have kept the projector but thrown away the slides made her feel sick.

'They're under there too, I think. In a tin.'

A Quality Street tin. The Quality Street tin that had been a button box when they were growing up, Piper thought. It was one of the things she'd loved about staying with Connie and Graeme. She would sit in the middle of the floor for literally hours, sorting the buttons into piles or just letting them run through her fingers.

'Wasn't this the button box?' she said now.

'Oh, I threw those away,' Connie said. 'No one replaces buttons any more. Do you want some toast?'

'I can do it,' Piper said, automatically.

'I bought some jam,' Connie said, frowning. 'But I can't remember where I put it.'

'Okay.' Piper followed her into the kitchen. 'Jam. I like jam.'

She opened the fridge and shifted around the random assortment of food: a dried-up lemon in the door, a packet of ham, an open tin of soup, the surface dotted with mould.

'This one's a bit past its best,' she said, taking it out and putting it on the counter, ready for the bin.

'Oh rubbish,' Connie said. 'I don't take any notice of all the sell-by and use-by dates. It's all a trick to make you spend more money. They didn't have them when I was young.'

'This one's mouldy though,' Piper told her. 'That's usually a bit of a clue.'

'You can just scrape that off,' Connie said.

And Piper suddenly remembered an argument when she was small. She and Holly staying with Connie. Connie slicing mould off the chunk of cheese she'd been about to use to make them cheese and crackers. Holly refusing to eat it, crying, saying she'd be sick. And Connie snapping and saying, 'Do it yourself then!' and stalking upstairs. Uncle Graeme had made them toast with honey instead.

'I don't think it's in here,' Piper said, crossing the kitchen to the cupboard above the kettle. She moved boxes of tea and jars of spices. The shelf was sticky and crunchy with salt.

'I sometimes put things on the top shelf,' Connie said, 'if I buy them before I need them.'

The top shelf was full of bags of flour, icing sugar, those little silver candy balls for cakes.

'Do you still bake?' Piper asked.

'I haven't. Not for a while. Can't work this oven.'

'Oh, there's honey!' Piper said. On the second shelf. 'How about honey?'

But when she unscrewed the lid, the honey was mixed with something brown. Marmite? Nutella? Gravy? There was no way of knowing.

'Biscuits!' Connie said so suddenly that Buster let out a small yap. 'Beryl brought me more of those blasted biscuits.'

*

When Piper first switched the projector on, the square of light was small, low on the wall behind Connie's sofa. She turned the dial on the front to make it bigger, but they had to find a pile of books to rest it on before they could get it centred on the wall.

Even the humming sound took Piper back to childhood. Her stomach twisted with a combination of nerves and excitement. She knew what was on the slides. And she wanted to see them. But she also didn't.

'Ready?' she asked Connie, lifting a slide out of the tin. Connie was ready. Piper wasn't sure she was.

She slotted the slide into the projector and clicked the button. The slide appeared on the wall, but out of focus and upside down.

Connie snorted. 'That always used to happen. I'd forgotten about that.'

Piper felt like she was holding her breath, like she was waiting for some great mystery to be revealed, as if the photo on the wall could change everything. Instead, when she got it in focus and the right way up, she saw herself and Holly, sitting on donkeys on the prom.

'I can't remember that at all,' she said, frowning. 'I've always said I've never been on a donkey. I went horse riding once with—'

With Rob. She didn't want to think about Rob.

Connie was holding slides up to the light, turning them the right way round and slotting them into the projector. She glanced up at the photo.

'That's just in front of the new flats. Where your fella lives.'

Piper hadn't realised, but she was right. The fort in the background. But the apartment block hadn't even been built back then.

'Remember Graeme's darkroom?' Connie said, still slotting slides.

Piper hadn't thought about the darkroom for years, but as soon as Connie mentioned it, she could smell the chemicals, feel the excitement of watching the photographs appear in the trays.

'He always had to be first with anything new,' Connie said. 'He hired a video camera once, for a party. This would be in the eighties. It was like a TV camera. Had to balance it on his shoulder and it had a separate thing... you know. The sound thing.'

'Microphone?' Piper guessed.

'That's it,' Connie said. 'On a stick. It picked up every sound in the room. Like in *Singing in the Rain*.'

She clicked onto the next slide. Christmas in Whitby. Piper was eight and Holly ten. They were sitting at the dining table in the cottage they'd hired, both wearing paper hats from crackers. Holly looked perfect, her hair in a neat bob, smiling at the camera. Piper's hat had fallen down over one eye and she was trying to look up from under it, her mouth half open, tongue poking out.

'She was a proper little madam even then,' Connie said.

She was, Piper thought. But she'd been Piper's best friend too. They'd go to bed in separate rooms and wake up in the same bed because one or both of them had had a nightmare. At primary school they'd obviously been in different classes, but they had the same friends and played together at playtime and lunch. It had been high school when things had changed and Piper still didn't know why.

The next slide showed Piper on her own, sitting on the sea wall, just near where she and Rob had sat and watched the sun come up after their aborted run. She wondered if he'd slept after she'd left or if he'd got up and run down the prom in the dark.

She wondered if he'd seen the rabbits. She wondered if he was asleep now or if he was thinking about her too.

The slide after that showed Holly and Piper with their parents, sitting what looked like halfway up a mountain. Piper had no idea where it could have been taken. She certainly didn't remember it, and they'd never been that much of an outdoorsy family.

'Where was this?' Piper asked Connie, still staring at the screen. Holly looked poised, smiling into the camera while also managing to look slightly conniving. Piper looked flushed, squinting and frowning into the sun. She could barely look at her parents.

'Connie?' Piper said again. 'Do you know where this was taken?'

She turned to look at her aunt. She was slumped in her seat, her head back against the cushions.

Piper's stomach clenched with fear. There was something about her aunt's face that just didn't look right. She grabbed her hand. 'Connie? Aunty Connie? Wake up? Please? Please.'

CHAPTER THIRTY-THREE

'She looks so much older,' Holly said. 'And smaller.'

She and Piper were sitting next to Connie's hospital bed, one on each side. Piper had been stroking Connie's hand, but her fingers were so thin, her skin so dry and papery, that she had to keep stopping. She fiddled with the ring Connie had given her instead, turning it round and round on her finger.

The previous night, Piper had first called an ambulance and then called Holly. Connie hadn't regained consciousness on the journey, or during the barrage of tests she'd been subjected to on arrival, or since.

Piper had stayed at Connie's flat, but had barely slept. Instead she'd curled up with Buster, listened to his heart beating and cried into his fur as he slept.

Holly had got the first train up in the morning, arriving at Connie's bedside looking tired and pale, her hair unwashed and face free of make-up. She'd held her arms out as if to hug Piper, before apparently remembering they didn't really do that any more and dropping down to kiss Connie's cheek instead.

'It's worse the longer she doesn't wake up,' Holly said. Even though Piper knew that; of course it was. 'What did the doctor say?'

'Nothing, really. Just that she's comfortable.' Piper picked Connie's hand up again. 'They've done a load of tests. I think they think it's a stroke.'

'That's what I thought,' Holly said. 'The way her mouth is...'

Connie's mouth was twisted. Only a little, but enough.

Piper nodded. She found herself blinking back tears again. She felt like she'd been either crying or trying not to cry for days now.

'Are you okay?' Holly asked Piper. 'Being here?'

Piper bit the inside of her cheek. She'd drawn blood doing the same last night, as soon as the ambulance had pulled up and she'd seen the light shining through the open doors. The antiseptic smell, the squeak of her shoes on the vinyl floor, the exhaustion on the faces of almost everyone she passed. She'd thought for a second she was going to faint. A nurse had brought her a plastic cup of strong sweet tea while she waited for Connie to be seen and she'd felt like it was the only thing tethering her to reality.

'No,' Piper said. 'But it's not like we have a choice.'

'No,' Holly said. 'I was thinking on the train… thank god you were there.'

Piper's throat burned. She nodded.

'Her neighbours would have found her,' Piper said. 'That's what I've been telling myself. Buster would've barked.'

Holly nodded. 'I feel horrible. I feel awful for not coming home.'

Piper shook her head. 'You're here now.'

Holly reached for her aunt's hand, but didn't pick it up, just rubbed her thumb over the loose skin on the back.

'Yeah,' she said. 'I suppose.'

Piper looked up at the clock. Visiting time was almost over. She didn't want to leave. She didn't want to leave and go back to Connie's and then get a phone call…

'Are you going to stay at Connie's?' she asked her sister.

'I thought I would, yeah. Do you think that's okay?'

Piper nodded. 'I'm staying there too.'

'Are you not staying at Robbie's?'

Piper shook her head. 'We're not that serious.'

Ignoring the look of confusion on her sister's face, she stood and rearranged the water jug and plastic cups on Connie's bedside table before opening the cupboard to make sure her things were still there. Not that she had much. Piper had brought her a couple of magazines for when she woke up. Because she had to wake up.

'Why not?' Holly asked. She was holding Connie's hand now, Piper noticed, and staring down at it, watching her thumb brush back and forth over the liver-spotted skin.

'Why not what?'

'You and Robbie. I thought—'

'Do we have to talk about this now?' Piper said.

'No. I didn't know it was a big thing. We can talk about it later, if you like.'

'There's nothing to talk about,' Piper said.

CHAPTER THIRTY-FOUR

They got the taxi home from the hospital in silence. The driver had Classic FM on loudly, so they probably couldn't have talked even if they'd wanted to. And Piper hadn't wanted to.

Outside Connie's flat, Holly said, 'Is there food? Or should I go and get something? Will Morrisons still be open?'

'There's food,' Piper said, heading up the path. 'But I'm not hungry.'

When Piper opened the door, Buster jumped up at her, before turning a few circles, his head thrown back with joy.

'Shit,' Piper said. 'Can you open the balcony door?'

She picked Buster up and rushed across the lounge, as Holly fiddled with the lock on the balcony door, but they didn't make it. Piper felt warm liquid dribbling down the front of her jeans. She put Buster outside anyway and looked down at herself, pulling her top away from her stomach.

'He always does that,' she told Holly. 'He's a ridiculous dog.'

Holly held out a packet of tissues and Piper pulled one out, dabbing at her jeans.

'Not for your jeans,' her sister said. 'For your face.'

Piper touched her cheek with the back of her hand and was surprised when it came back wet. She hadn't even realised she was crying.

'I'm going to make tea and toast,' Holly said. 'Take your clothes off and put them in the wash.' She stopped and squeezed Piper's arm quickly. 'She's going to be okay.'

Piper nodded and headed for the bedroom.

*

It turned out that in packing so quickly, Piper had brought an almost useless selection of clothes, but thankfully she had managed to include a long-sleeved T-shirt. She peeled off her wet jeans and top, showered quickly in Connie's feeble shower and took her washing through to the kitchen.

Holly was on the sofa in the living room, Buster next to her and two mugs of tea and a plate of toast with jam on the coffee table in front of her.

'Thank you,' Piper said, sitting on the other side of Buster and reaching for a tea. Her hands were still shaking. They'd been shaking all day. She pulled her legs up on the sofa and put a cushion in her lap.

'Do we need to talk about—' Holly said.

'Rob told me he's falling in love with me,' Piper interrupted.

'Fuck me.' Holly turned to face her sister on the sofa. 'What did you say?'

Piper shook her head. 'I freaked. I left. I came back here.'

'Wow. You don't feel the same way?'

Piper frowned. 'It's too soon! He's being ridiculous.'

'You've been seeing each other for a while though, haven't you? I thought you liked him.'

'I do.' Piper reached for a slice of toast. 'I really like him. He's great. He's funny and kind and hot as hell. But—'

'But? How's the sex?'

Piper shook her head. 'Unbelievable.'

'I have to say, you're rapidly losing my sympathy.' Holly reached for a slice of toast too and moaned as she bit into it. 'I can't believe I denied myself this for so long.'

'But,' Piper continued. 'He lives here. I live in London. He's not going to move to London and I'm sure as shit not moving back here, so—'

'Have you asked him?' Holly said.

'Asked him what?'

'If he'd move to London.'

'Of course not.'

'Why not?'

'Because.'

Holly raised one eyebrow.

'Because why would he?'

'Because he's in love with you.'

Piper shook her head.

'I saw his post on Facebook,' Holly said.

Piper was actually surprised. As far as she knew, Holly rarely, if ever, went on Facebook. She said it was politically and morally reprehensible. And crammed with photos of the cats and babies of people she didn't care about.

'Oh yeah?' Piper said.

'A friend sent it to me.'

'Sent you what?'

'A screenshot. Of the photo he posted.'

'Ah,' Piper said. 'Yeah. That was a bit shit.'

'It was horrendous. But I didn't mean that. The photo he posted. And his comment. I could tell even then that he was into you. And you looked so happy in the photo. And so completely yourself. It took my breath away a bit.'

Piper didn't even know what to say. She didn't think Holly had ever said anything like that to her before.

'I never should have married James,' she said. 'I knew it wasn't right. I knew I didn't love him. Not like I should have loved him. But everything else was – seemed – perfect, so I ignored it. It was the biggest mistake I ever made. If you think you could be happy with Rob – and I know you do – you shouldn't risk losing him because you're scared.'

'I'm not scared,' Piper said.

'It's braver to risk it than to avoid it, you know. I know you think you're protecting yourself. But you can protect yourself too well. And end up with nothing.'

'Christ,' Piper said. She stared down at Buster, pushing her hand into his fur.

'No, listen. I went through the same thing you did. I know we've never really talked about it. I get that you probably don't want to talk about it now, but you know I understand, right? And if you ever do want to talk—'

'I don't,' Piper said.

'Okay. And you don't want to talk about me and Matt either?'

'No. But I'm pissed off.'

'I get that,' Holly said. 'I don't blame you.'

CHAPTER THIRTY-FIVE

Piper woke up in the night and turned over to find Holly on the other side of Connie's bed. She was on her side facing Piper, fast asleep. Piper watched her for a while in the dim light from the streetlamp outside. She was really still. Piper shuffled across the bed, leaning closer, until she was confident her sister was in fact breathing and she could go back to sleep.

'You awake?' Holly asked what seemed like minutes later.

'What time is it?' Piper groaned, throwing her arm over her eyes.

She felt the mattress move as Holly presumably reached for her phone. 'Eight.'

'I'd better take Buster out.' She sat up and stretched. 'They'd have phoned us in the night, right? If she'd died.'

'I don't know,' Holly said. 'I'll phone now.'

Piper got up, took her clothes out of the dryer, got dressed and fed Buster, the sound of her sister's voice in the other room, on the phone to the hospital, making her stomach churn.

'She's awake,' Holly said, coming through to the lounge. 'They said she's doing well. She asked for you.'

Piper's eyes filled again and she grabbed Holly's arm, pulling her into a hug. 'Oh my god.'

'I know,' Holly said. 'Want to go and see her when you get back from taking Buster out?'

At the sound of his name, Buster whimpered and wriggled on the spot.

'I'll book a cab,' Holly said.

*

Piper bought a latte in Starbucks and walked down to the beach, crunching over the shells. While Buster ran around her in ever-increasing circles, occasionally stopping to bark at a seagull or chase another dog's ball, Piper stared out to sea. Connie was alive. She was going to be okay. And Piper had hugged Holly without even thinking about it. She couldn't even remember when they'd stopped hugging. Or why. It was ridiculous really.

Once she'd finished her coffee, she turned back up the beach, yelling for Buster to join her. By the time she got to the prom, he let her snap his lead back on and started tugging her towards home.

'Not that way,' she told him, steering him in the opposite direction. 'Not yet.'

*

'Hey,' Rob said when he opened the door. 'And Buster too.'

Buster darted between Rob's legs and immediately started whirling and wriggling.

'Dude, seriously?' Piper said. 'You've literally just been.'

Rob grabbed the dog and half-ran across his living room, sliding open the balcony door and depositing Buster outside.

'I am so sorry,' Piper said, as they both watched Buster pee on Rob's tiled floor. 'I didn't think he'd have any left in him.'

Once he was done, Buster darted past the two of them back into the flat and jumped up on the sofa.

'Yeah, you make yourself at home,' Rob told him.

'I'm sorry,' Piper said again.

'It's not a problem,' Rob said. 'I always thought my sofa needed that wet dog smell.'

'Not about that,' Piper said. 'But also about that, obviously. I meant about the other night. For leaving like that.'

'For leaving like that and then ignoring my texts?' Rob said.

Piper shook her head and, to her embarrassment, started to cry. 'Connie had a stroke.'

CHAPTER THIRTY-SIX

'I had a thing,' Connie said, gesturing with her good hand, the one that hadn't been curled into a fist by the stroke. 'A mini stroke thing. They call it a... something. Tee something.'

'TIA,' Holly said. She was sitting next to Connie's bed, opposite Piper.

'I didn't tell you girls because I didn't want you to worry. And I didn't want to think about it.'

Her speech was slow and slurred, but nowhere near as bad as Piper had been expecting. The nurse who had met them in the hallway had said Connie was as strong as an ox – she'd woken up first thing and immediately demanded tea and breakfast and for someone to call 'her girls'.

'You did tell me,' Piper said, frowning.

'Did I?' Connie said. 'Well I didn't mean to.'

Piper didn't think this was a TIA at all. She'd done some googling and she was pretty sure this was an actual stroke. But the staff wouldn't tell her anything, telling her to ask her aunt, and Connie seemed determined to pretend it was nothing serious. Piper could accept that. For now at least.

'How's Buster?' Connie asked, straining as she tried to shuffle up against her pillows.

While Piper told her aunt about Buster disgracing himself at Rob's earlier, Holly stood up, helped Connie to lean forward, rearranged her pillows, and then lowered her back down. Connie smiled at her, gratefully.

'You look just the same,' she told her. 'I've missed your face.'

Piper watched Holly's face crumple a little, but then she composed herself. 'I'm sorry. I let things get on top of me a bit. But I'm sorting it all out now.'

Connie patted her hand. 'You're a good girl.'

She took a sip of her tea and Piper watched some of it dribble out of the corner of her mouth and run down her neck to the neckline of her pale blue nighty. Holly reached over and dabbed it with a tissue.

'You don't have to keep coming,' Connie told Piper, her eyes closed. 'I'm alright.'

'Of course we're going to keep coming,' Piper said. 'Have they said how long you're going to be in?'

'I don't think so. But it's expensive. All the taxis.'

'Rob brought us,' Holly said.

Connie opened her eyes and looked straight at Piper. 'He's a good lad, that one. You should keep him.'

Piper swallowed and nodded.

'And he likes big girls?' She blinked.

'He likes me,' Piper said.

'That's good,' Connie said and closed her eyes again.

*

'Do you think Rob would drop me at the station?' Holly asked in the lift on the way back down.

'I'm sure he will, yeah.'

'I wish I could stay,' Holly said. 'But I've just got so much shit to sort out at home.'

'I think I'm going to stay the rest of the week,' Piper said. 'Work said to take as much time as I need, so...'

'That's good.'

The lift doors opened and they stepped out and to the side, out of the way, but neither of them made a move towards the coffee shop where they knew Rob was waiting.

'When did we stop talking?' Holly said.

'I don't know. I was thinking about that too.'

'It was before Mum and Dad though, right?'

Piper nodded. 'But that didn't help.'

'No. It was weird. I remembered this morning how I used to get into your bed in the night.'

'What, after you got into my bed in the night?' Piper smiled.

'Yeah. I don't even remember getting up. I never did when we were kids either.'

'It wasn't just you,' Piper said. 'I did it too.'

Holly leaned back against the wall and then jerked upright again, glancing back over her shoulder.

'I think the walls are probably clean,' Piper said.

'Ugh, I know. It's just hospitals. They give me the heebs.'

Piper laughed. 'Right?'

'We should go and find Rob. I need to get my train.'

As they walked to the cafe, Holly said, 'I woke up in the night and you were so still I had to check you were still breathing.'

Piper stopped walking – she heard someone tut behind her – and stared at her sister. 'I did the same thing!'

'You did not!'

'I did! I almost poked you. But I thought you'd be pissed off if I woke you up.'

Holly grinned. 'I would've been. But oh my god. We're both so fucked up.'

Piper bumped her sister with her shoulder. 'I think we're doing okay.'

*

After they'd dropped Holly at the station, Piper suggested she and Rob go out for lunch. They headed back up the motorway, 'One More Night' by Phil Collins blaring out of the tinny speakers, while Piper laughed and tried not to sing along.

'Do you know where you want to go?' Rob asked, as they passed the allotments where they'd ridden his aunt's horse.

Piper craned her neck to look down on them, but she couldn't see much apart from plastic sheeting and sheds.

'Surprise me,' she said.

'So... the big Tesco?'

'I meant a good surprise.' She hid her smile against the window.

The next song was, inevitably, 'Mr Brightside' and this time Piper didn't even consider not singing along. Rob drummed on the steering wheel and opened both front windows to let the cool air rush into the car.

'I don't know what it is about that song,' he said once it was over and they'd pulled off the motorway. 'It used to remind me of all of us on the prom, titting about. Then the reunion.' He glanced at her and then back at the road. 'And now this. In the car. With you.'

'It's a good song,' she said.

Rob had driven through West Kirby and was heading up the hill towards... Piper wasn't sure where.

'Where are we going?'

'There's this place my dad used to take me,' Rob said. 'A pub. On the river. I've tried to find it before and missed it completely, but I think I can find it...'

They drove through Caldy, Thurstaston, Heswall, singing a lot and talking a little. But Piper mostly looked out of the window.

'We used to come here with my parents when we were little,' she said. 'We'd drive around and look at the big houses, pick the one we'd live in when we were rich.'

'Yeah?'

'At one point, my dad would always say, "That's Paul McCartney's house." It was always a different house.'

Rob laughed. 'We saw him in the pub once. On Christmas Eve. He was sitting there with friends, drinking and laughing like a normal person. I mean, he is a normal person, I guess. But I just kept thinking, "That's Paul McCartney. From The Beatles." I was scared to go to the loo in case he came in and I said something inappropriate or tried to hug him or something.'

'Must be so weird to be that famous. People just going "Holy shit" when they see you. That's what I used to think I wanted. To go to London and just become super famous. I used to interview myself in my head, all that.'

'What did you want to do?' Rob asked. He'd slowed down now and was peering through the windscreen, presumably looking for a sign.

'Have you not got a sat nav?' Piper asked.

'No. Used to. But I kept looking at it instead of the road. I was on a roundabout once and I looked at the screen and there was my car, going round the roundabout. And I was thinking, "Hey, look! My car! Going round a roundabout!" and I crashed into the car in front.'

'You did not!'

'I did. I'm an idiot. Oh hey, there's the turn-off.'

He pulled off to the right down a wide road sloping down to the river, with bungalows on either side. He turned and turned again, down lanes with fields on one side, smaller, white-painted houses on the other, past a car park and finally down a bumpy track.

'How does anyone ever find this place?' Piper asked.

'No idea,' Rob said. 'But see that house there?' He pointed out of his window to a mock Tudor mansion half hidden behind tall gates.

'Yeah?'

'Paul McCartney lives there.'

Piper let out a bark of laughter and Rob grinned at her as he turned off the road and into the restaurant's car park.

*

'I love your body,' Rob said later, back at his flat, his mouth somewhere around Piper's ribcage.

'Pfft.'

Rob crawled up the bed, leaning over her to look at her face. 'Did you just say "pfft"?'

Piper shook her head, closing her eyes. 'I didn't mean to. It just came out.'

'You don't believe I love your body? Because I feel like I've been quite clear...' He kissed her shoulder. 'About...' The dip of her throat. 'How...' The top of a breast. 'Much...' The curve of her belly.

'Okay okay,' Piper said, curling away from his mouth.

'I wasn't finished,' Rob said, pulling her back towards him and mouthing down her side in the direction of her hip.

'I do believe it,' she said. 'Sort of. Mostly.'

Rob stopped kissing and touching and moved back up to lie next to her, his eyebrows furrowed.

'I don't understand. I mean, I've read your blog. You're so confident. And you know you're completely fucking gorgeous, right?'

Piper shook her head again. Embarrassingly, her eyes were pricking with tears.

'You called me chubby.' She hadn't actually meant to say that.

'What? When?'

Piper kept her eyes closed. 'Years ago. When we were kids. When I got stuck up that tree and—'

The bed was shaking. The bed was shaking because Rob was laughing, his face pressed into her neck.

'Oh what the fuck?!' Piper said.

'I'm sorry,' Rob said. 'Have you seriously been holding that against me all this time?'

Piper opened her eyes and stared at the white ceiling for a second before rolling onto her side to face him.

'Yes.'

His face became serious the instant he saw that she was serious. 'Piper. Fuck. I didn't—'

'I know you didn't. I know that. But you don't understand how that felt for me. You were the only one who never treated me like the fat girl. For ages, I sort of felt like you didn't know. As if you hadn't noticed. I used to sometimes let myself think that you liked me and then I'd honestly think "oh but it's because he doesn't know I'm fat". Which I know is ridiculous because you were right there. I knew you could see me! But that's how I felt. Everyone else made little comments. Or I caught them looking at me and I knew what they were thinking. But that never happened with you. Until that day.'

'I'm sorry,' Rob said. 'I don't even remember exactly what I said—'

Piper smiled. 'Yeah. But I do. I always have. You said, "I like chubby girls better anyway."'

'Oh god,' Rob said. 'That. That was dickhead me's idea of a compliment. I wanted you to know that I liked you—'

'Anyway,' Piper interrupted. 'You wanted me to know that you liked me anyway. Even though I was fat.'

'No,' Rob said, his forehead furrowing. 'That's not it. I don't think? Even then I liked it. I liked how you looked. I used to think about touching you and how soft you'd feel.'

Piper dipped her head, the crown against his chest. 'You did not.'

He stroked the back of her neck. 'I did. Remember when I got off with Claire?'

'Vividly,' Piper said drily.

'I kept thinking about how it would have been better with you.'

'Because she had tiny tits.'

Rob laughed. 'Not just that. But yeah, also that.'

Piper straightened up to look at him. 'Have you slept with other fat women?'

He grimaced. 'We're having this conversation?'

'Apparently.'

'Yes. I've slept with other fat women. And thin women. I've slept with women of various shapes and sizes.'

'Bigger than me?'

'Yes.'

'Who?'

'I mean, you don't know her,' Rob said.

Piper rolled her eyes. 'Describe her to me.'

'It was one night. On a teacher training course in a really shitty hotel. We all went out and got drunk. She was funny and sexy and an amazing dancer.'

'Like Fat Monica.'

'Who the fuck is Fat Monica?'

'Sorry. *Friends.* Forgot. Carry on.'

'That was it. We slept together. We didn't keep in touch.'

'What was her name?'

'Rachel.'

'Are you taking the piss?'

'No! That was her name!'

'Okay. Tell me about the one in Ibiza. With the stupid name. Flounder.'

Rob laughed. 'Belle.'

'Sure.'

'She was thin.'

'How thin?'

'Christ, I don't know! I'm not in the habit of asking women I sleep with for their measurements or BMI or whatever. Why does it matter?'

Piper shook her head. 'I'm sorry. It doesn't. I just—'

'I want you. I think you're incredibly hot and sexy. I love your body whether you believe me or not. And I'm sorry that dickhead teen me made you feel like shit for even a second, let alone for, like, fifteen years.'

Piper moved closer, hooking her foot around his ankle.

'If I could go back in time,' Rob said. 'I'd tell him to tell you how much he fancied you. That he thought about you all the time. That some of his earliest wanking—'

'Okay,' Piper said, moving the rest of the way and shutting him up with a kiss.

*

'Did you really?' she said, later, her head on his chest, his hand stroking the dip in her side down over her hip. He seemed to like that bit of her the best – she should ask him about it.

'Did I really what?' Rob asked.

'Did you really wank thinking about me? Back then?'

Rob laughed, his chest shaking under her head.

'Of course. But don't get too over-excited, I wanked over everything back then. I was like the Victorians with the table legs.'

Piper laughed. 'I can imagine.'

'Unless you've had to hide an erection in a newsagent because you heard the words "Holly Willoughby" on the radio, you really can't.'

Piper laughed again. 'It must be a nightmare.'

'Oh it is,' Rob said. 'Or it was back then. I don't mind it so much now.'

Piper hooked her leg over his thighs. 'Again?'

Rob rolled her over. 'Again.'

CHAPTER THIRTY-SEVEN

Connie was out of hospital by Wednesday. Her speech was still a little slurred and her hand curled – she'd been told to exercise it with a tennis ball, which was turning out to be tricky since Buster kept nicking it – but she was otherwise almost back to her old self.

She'd been telling Piper to go home pretty much on the hour, every hour.

'I've got the week off,' Piper told her. 'I'll go home on Friday.'

'Go and stay with your fella then,' Connie suggested, washing dishes that Piper had offered to do. 'I don't want you under my feet all the time.'

Piper rolled her eyes. 'I'm going for a drink with him later. But I'll be back. I don't want to leave you on your own yet.'

'I'm fine on my own,' Connie said. 'I've been on my own for years. And this is exactly why I didn't—' She turned back to the sink and turned on the hot tap.

'Why you didn't tell us about the mini strokes?' Connie had admitted to having had two earlier in the year.

'I don't like a lot of fuss,' she said now without turning round. 'Beryl and Jim and you and Holly. I'm fine. Look.' She held up her curled hand and flexed her thumb at Piper. 'Be glad I can't straighten my middle finger.'

Piper laughed and caught her aunt smiling before she turned back to the dishes.

'It's not for me,' she said, crossing the room and wrapping her arms around Connie's waist. 'I'll worry about you if I'm not here.'

Connie wriggled and shook her off. 'I'm old, but I'm not dead. You and your sister have got your own lives. It would be lovely if you could come home more, but I know you'll be doing that anyway because of whatshisname.'

'Rob,' Piper said.

'That's him. So go on. Bugger off.'

*

'Where did you even get this?' Piper said an hour or so later on Rob's balcony, staring at the small cassette in her hand. She couldn't think when she'd last seen one. Had forgotten the size of them, how light they were. She poked a finger into one of the holes and felt the tiny spikes, remembered twisting the tape back in when it had somehow spooled out.

'I've got my sources,' Rob said. He was sitting on the bench, shirtless, his skin golden in the early evening sun. Piper was finding it very distracting.

'eBay?' she asked.

'Argos.'

She laughed. 'Wow. Who knew.' She turned it over. Rob's handwriting on the label: *For Piper*.

'How am I going to listen to it though?'

'Well I thought about that.' He reached into the bag and handed her a small box.

She laughed. She was tearing up. 'This must've been eBay.'

'It was, yeah.'

It was a Walkman.

'I got batteries,' Rob said. 'I thought you could listen on the train? Or, you know, wherever. I'm trying not to be a control freak about it.'

'This is perfect,' Piper said, leaning over to kiss him. 'I love it.'

*

On the train, Piper turned the Walkman over in her hands. She liked the chunky solidity of it. Rob had driven her to the station and kissed her on the platform, while hurrying passengers tutted and one guy barged them with his rucksack. But she hadn't wanted to leave. Or she'd wished Rob was going home with her. She wasn't quite sure which.

She'd bought herself a mini bottle of wine and she poured a (plastic) glass before putting headphones in and pressing play.

The first song was 'I Bet You Look Good on the Dancefloor', followed by 'Valerie' by The Zutons, which she remembered dancing to in a pub not long before she left for London. She closed her eyes and thought about Rob, the reunion, finding him again after all these years and him actually liking her back. She still couldn't quite believe it. Except she could because he made it very clear. Her stomach fluttered as 'One Day Like This' started and she remembered them dancing to it at the reunion and then singing it in the car. She was happier singing in the car with Rob than she'd been having sex with some previous boyfriends.

She'd almost finished her first glass of wine when the next song started and the opening guitar riff made her heart race instantly. At first she wasn't sure why and then she realised: it was 'Everlong' by Foo Fighters. Her dad's favourite song. Her dad's favourite song about finding someone and singing with them and falling in love. She poured the rest of the wine into the glass and drank it as she listened to the song all the way through. She remembered her dad and Rob talking about music once at a party in someone's garden. Her dad had liked Rob. Everyone liked Rob.

She took her headphones off and put the Walkman back in her bag, tapping Rob's number on her mobile as she made her way to the end of the carriage.

'Hey,' he said, answering.

His voice in her ear made her stomach flutter.

To Piper's relief, there was no one else between the carriages. She leaned against the wall and looked at her reflection in the window. It wasn't the most glamorous or romantic place for this conversation, but she couldn't wait.

'I just called,' she said into the phone, 'to say I love you.'

CHAPTER THIRTY-EIGHT

When Piper got home, Matt was waiting for her with a bottle of wine, a bunch of flowers and a Thai takeaway. He was wide-eyed and unshaven, his hair all over the place.

'I've only been away a week,' Piper said instead of hello. 'How are you feral?'

'I took the day off work to clean the flat and get stuff ready.'

He was still hanging back a little, standing by the table, hadn't grabbed her and hugged her like he usually would. Piper looked around. The fibre-optic light Connie had given her was still in pride of place. The wooden deer stood on the sideboard at the far end of the room. A blanket made by her mum that Connie had repaired and cleaned was folded and arranged over the back of the sofa.

Piper dropped her bag and crossed the room to wrap her arms around him.

'I'm so sorry, Pips,' he said, squeezing her back.

'Don't call me Pips,' she said into the side of his neck. 'You absolute dick.'

She felt tears burning the backs of her eyes and pushed him away before pulling him back in again and giving him one more squeeze.

'Wine?' he said.

'Please. A pint.'

Matt poured wine and took the lids off the takeaway cartons while Piper headed into her bedroom to strip off the clothes she'd basically been wearing all week, supplemented only by some joggers and a jumper she'd grabbed from Primark between hospital visits. In her pyjamas, her hair pulled back off her make-up free face, she joined Matt on the other end of the sofa – the food spread out on the coffee table, Troye Sivan's *Blue Neighbourhood* slinking from Matt's laptop – and picked up her wine.

She'd spoken to Matt a couple of times during the week, but she hadn't had the energy to talk about what had happened with Holly. She'd told him that they were okay, and that she and Holly were okay, but that was pretty much all.

'So Jack dumped me,' Matt started. 'For being old.'

'Fuck off,' Piper said, appalled.

'Right? I know. And I felt like shit about it. So that day Holly came round, I'd come home early from work feeling sorry for myself. I was going to have a bath and get pissed and do something inadvisable via Grindr.'

'Standard Friday night,' Piper said, poking his thigh with her bare toes.

'But then Holly turned up. And she was miserable as fuck too. So we opened the wine and we talked about how shit we both are at relationships and then, you know, you came home and yelled at us.'

'I know. I was just… surprised.'

Matt covered his mouth as a laugh burst out of him. 'You were fucking horrified.'

Piper drank some more wine. 'I was, yeah. I never would've put the two of you together. And I'd just got the new job—'

'Yeah, I need to hear all about that.'

'Nothing much to tell yet, but yeah. So I was all excited and I bought Prosecco and thought me and you would get pissed and have a laugh and maybe go out and dance after and instead I was faced with my stuck-up sister and her sex hair.'

'I can see why that would be upsetting for you,' Matt said in his fake therapy voice. He shuffled up the sofa and reached over to the table, to pile some of the starters – chicken satay, tofu, prawn crackers – onto a plate.

'But also I realised something, on the way home. I think part of it was that you've always told me everything. You always share every bit of your life with me. So it freaked me out when I thought you had this secret. Of course, it made it so much fucking worse that it was my sister.'

Matt stared at her, a prawn cracker halfway to his mouth. 'You know what I was thinking about? When you weren't replying to my texts and I was conducting devastating arguments with you in the shower?'

Piper winced. 'Go on.'

'You don't share your life with me like that. I mean, most of it you do. Your London life. But not the rest of it. I thought it was because it was Holly. And you like to keep me and her separate as much as possible. But then I thought, like, I've never been home with you. And I'd like to. And I'd love to meet Rob.'

Piper nodded. Her stomach felt hollow with nerves, rather than hunger. 'You're right. I always felt like I left it all behind. But I didn't really. Of course I fucking didn't.'

Matt reached over and rubbed the side of her calf. 'Hey, I do it too. I think everyone does a bit. But I feel like you do it a lot.'

Piper nodded. 'And you know what, it was actually really good being home with Holly.' She leaned over to get her own food. 'We talked a bit. We even fucking hugged.'

'Jesus,' Matt said.

'I know. So, like… I mean if you and her…' She picked up a duck spring roll and swiped it through the hoisin sauce before shoving it in her mouth.

Matt grinned at her, wiggling his feet into the cushions. 'Are you giving us your blessing?'

'Oh god,' Piper said, her mouth still full. 'Fuck off.'

'No, it's amazing. Are you sure you don't want to know my intentions?'

Piper gave him the finger and then reached for another spring roll.

'We've talked,' Matt said. 'Me and Holly. It was just that one time. She's not really in a place to start anything up. And you know me: total slag.'

'You're not a slag,' Piper said. 'You've just got a lot of love to give.'

'To a lot of people! I know, right?' He grinned.

'Thank you for putting the stuff out,' she said, gesturing at the wooden deer. 'My parents' stuff.'

'It looks good, right? You should bring more back next time you go home.'

'I might,' Piper said. 'Yeah.'

*

'I'm moving back home,' Holly said at brunch on Sunday morning. 'I'm going to move in with Connie.'

'You're not,' Piper said. 'Seriously?'

Holly nodded. 'I've never been happy here. In London. But you are, Piper. And you shouldn't give that up.'

'I didn't know you weren't happy,' Piper said. 'I always thought you loved it.'

Holly shook her head. 'I loved my job and the house and James, but I never loved living here. Not the way you do. And now I don't have James or the job or the house… there's no reason for me to stay. I don't want to stay.'

'But you go home even less than I do!' Piper said. 'You can really see yourself living there?'

'I don't know,' Holly said. 'Maybe? I mean… it's not exactly what I'd imagined myself doing. Living with an eighty-year-old woman in the town I grew up in. But she needs someone. And I need some time to work out where I go from here.'

'What did Connie say?'

'You know Connie. She said not to move back on her account. But I think she was relieved. I think she's been a bit scared. And she's sick of Beryl calling in all the time. And if it doesn't work out there then I can move out and find somewhere else. But I'm going to start there, at least.'

'I can't believe it,' Piper said. 'I'm going to miss you.'

Holly laughed. 'Now I can't believe that.'

Piper smiled. 'Maybe a few months ago I wouldn't have done. But it's been better lately, hasn't it? We've been getting closer.'

Holly nodded. 'I'll miss that. But you're going to come home more.'

'I am.'

'And I can always come down and stay with you. I'm fine visiting London, I just don't want to live here.'

'You know what they say? Tired of London…'

Holly rolled her eyes. 'Living in London was making me tired of life. I want something else. And James is buying me out of the house so I'll have time and money to work out what that might be.'

*

They walked back to the Tube together afterwards.

'I've been reading your blog,' Holly said, ducking her head, as if she was embarrassed. 'I should've been reading it all along, I know. But I just—'

'It's fine,' Piper said. 'It doesn't matter.'

'It's really good. And I want to tell you something.' They waited at the traffic lights, both of them staring straight ahead. 'I went to the doctor,' Holly said. She lowered her voice. 'I actually went to get the morning after pill because me and Matt—'

'Jesus Christ,' Piper said, shaking her head. 'I don't even want to know. Plus there's condoms in the bathroom, for fuck's sake.'

'Right. Sorry.' They crossed the road. 'Okay, so I went to the doctor and my blood pressure was really high. And they weren't concerned. Like, at all? They said maybe it was stress, but they didn't ask about exercise or diet and the nurse actually said that I didn't look like someone with high blood pressure so it was probably just a blip. And then I went back – after I'd handed my notice in – and it was fine, so, you know. But it made me think… they literally decided I must be healthy just because I'm slim. And that's bullshit.'

Piper was lost for words. Her throat felt too tight to swallow, but she needed to swallow or she was scared she might cry.

'Pipes?' Holly said, her forehead furrowed with concern.

'I'm okay,' Piper managed to say. 'I just… it means a lot to me. That you would realise that.'

'I feel like a shit for not realising before, to be honest,' Holly said. 'I remember you saying that you can't tell someone's health by looking at them and I kind of agreed. But I also kind of felt like obviously someone fatter would be less healthy. Like that was just beyond all question. And that's just wrong. And it's, like, obviously wrong? Everyone knows thin people who eat like shit and do no exercise, but it's like it's okay just because they're thin. I mean… what the fuck *is* that?'

Holly looked so indignant, so appalled, that Piper laughed. 'I know. But it is hard, I know. All this stuff is so ingrained. And reinforced everywhere. I'm not really surprised that people believe it. But it's not true.'

'And it's not just that. I was a dick to you about your weight. When we were teens. And probably after? But you're so brave. I knew you were. Like you left and went to London and you were so young. But you wanted to do it and you just did it and I didn't think I ever could.'

'But you did.'

'I did it once I could control everything. Once I had a job and a place and—'

'You still did it. And I went to uni, I didn't just go with like a hanky on a stick and a fucking song in my heart.'

'But you still did it,' Holly said. 'And it was really brave. I just wanted to tell you that.'

Piper nodded. 'Thank you. I appreciate it.'

'And I think… I think maybe losing Mum and Dad made us both less brave. Scared to take risks. But I really think we should, you know? We have to.'

Piper nodded. 'I'm definitely going to try.'

CHAPTER THIRTY-NINE

'Are you excited?' Matt asked Piper. 'Nervous?'

'About the launch or about you meeting Rob?'

Matt grinned. 'Both.'

The launch for Bitter/Sweet was taking place on a super-yacht moored on the Thames. Juliette had found it, but Piper had done everything else, arranging the party and the press conference that would take place later, after the girls had zipped off down the river in a speedboat. Everyone left on the yacht would go on partying without them. Piper had always enjoyed her job, but since moving to Press she absolutely loved it.

'I'm excited about the launch and nervous about you meeting Rob.'

Matt wrapped one arm around her shoulder and squeezed. 'I'm sure I'm going to love him.' He raised one eyebrow. 'Maybe a little too much... '

Piper rolled her eyes. 'You know Holly's coming too?'

'Yep. I'm planning to hide in one of the lifeboats.'

'Matt!'

'Nah, it's fine. We've talked. We're cool.'

'Holly's never been cool with anything in her life.'

'Sleeping with me changes a person.'

'I can only imagine.'

Matt hooked his chin over Piper's shoulder and squeezed her again. 'Have I told you how fucking proud I am?'

'Once or twice, yeah.' But she was beaming.

Piper tipped her head back and looked at her reflection in the gold mirrored ceiling. She looked happy

'Don't look up!' Matt said. 'You'll see my bald spot.'

'You haven't got a bald spot, for god's sake.'

'Not yet,' Matt said. 'But I could have.'

Her phone buzzed with a text from Rob telling her he was downstairs. She told him to come up to the first floor and turned towards the lifts, that were just behind them in the foyer. Her stomach fluttered with nerves as she watched the lift disappear, knowing that when it came back up, Rob would be in it.

'Oh my god,' Matt said. 'Look at you!'

'Shut up,' Piper said.

'You are so smitten.'

The lift stopped and the doors opened to reveal Rob in black jeans and a long-sleeved black sweater, sunglasses pushed up on his head.

'Oh my god,' Matt said. 'Look at him!'

Ignoring Matt, Piper walked over to the lifts and straight into Rob's arms.

'Hi,' he said into her hair.

'I've missed you.' She turned her head to kiss his neck, breathing in the scent of his skin.

'Me too,' Rob said. 'Are you excited or nervous?'

Piper laughed. 'Both. And Matt just asked me the same thing.'

'I'm going to assume Matt's the guy staring at us at the bottom of the stairs?'

Piper laughed and kissed Rob quickly, before taking his hand and leading him over to Matt.

'So,' Rob said, holding his hand out to Matt. 'At last we meet.'

Matt let out a bark of laughter and shook Rob's hand.

'This one's a keeper,' he told Piper.

'Jesus Christ,' Piper said. 'Can you go and get drinks and stop showing me up?'

Matt kissed her cheek, took everyone's drink orders and headed over to the bar. Piper introduced Rob to Juliette and John.

'Is that Holly?' Rob asked Piper.

Piper turned to see her sister coming out of the lift. She was wearing a tea dress and ballerina flats and looked happier and more relaxed than Piper had seen her for years. Possibly ever.

'She looks good,' Matt said.

'Don't even think about it.'

Holly reached the three of them and Rob immediately pulled her into a hug.

'You look exactly the same,' he said.

'You don't.' Holly looked up at him. He was at least a foot taller than her. 'Bloody hell.'

'Fit as fuck, isn't he?' Matt said.

'Piper's warned me about you,' Rob told him, smiling.

'Me too,' Holly said. 'But too late.'

'Oh my god.' Matt took a swig of his gin. 'Where's that lifeboat?'

They were interrupted by Anthony, the head of the label, clearing his throat on the stairs.

The chatter stopped and everyone looked up at him.

'First of all I want to thank everyone for coming. All of us at Infinite Plays are extremely excited to introduce you to our new signing. We're sure you're going to love them as much as we do.' He glanced over his shoulder up the stairs. 'They would be pissed at me trying to speak on their behalf, so I'll let them introduce themselves. This is Bitter/Sweet.'

The girls walked down the wide staircase, the light from the enormous chandelier reflecting off their glittery dresses. All three looked confident and poised and like they'd been doing this for years, not that it was their first public appearance and they'd only bought the dresses that morning in Topshop, Oxford Circus after they'd decided what they'd planned to wear wasn't vibrant enough.

'They look amazing,' Matt whispered into Piper's ear. 'I'm into it.'

The girls gave a short, excited speech – talking over the top of each other and spontaneously bursting into an acapella version of the song that the label was thinking of making their first single, and then everyone moved into the bar and out onto the deck.

'This is fantastic,' Rob said, curling his arms around Piper's waist, as they looked out over the river to Canary Wharf and the O2. 'I'm so proud of you.'

'I'm proud of myself actually,' Piper said.

'You should be.'

Matt and Holly joined them at the railing and Holly held out her glass. 'I think we should make a toast.'

Piper held up her glass.

'To Piper,' Holly said. 'Her new job. And her new-ish man.'

Piper laughed, looking up at Rob.

'And to your new life too,' Piper said. 'In our old home town.'

They clinked their glasses and watched the girls speed off down the Thames, shrieking with laughter and waving bottles of champagne.

Piper half wished she could have gone with them. But she was also completely happy exactly where she was.

CHAPTER FORTY

'I brought you something,' Rob said, lifting a medium-sized cardboard box out of a B&Q carrier bag. The box was for a lampshade.

'It's not a lampshade,' Rob said. 'This was the only box it fit in.'

'Can I open it now?' Piper asked, carrying it over to her small dining table.

'Course.'

'Oh wait, do you want a tea or something first?'

'No, I'm fine. Thanks. Open it.' Rob grinned at her.

'You don't want to go to bed first?' Piper said, raising one eyebrow. 'While Matt's out?'

'Yes. Shit. Leave it.' He reached for her hand and she stretched hers out to take his. 'No, I'm joking. I can wait five minutes. Open it.'

Piper had to take a second to internally shake herself since mentally she was already on her way to the bedroom and reaching for Rob's clothes. She didn't know how he did this to her. Just the suggestion of sex and her brain turned to marshmallow fluff.

She stared down at the box. *Open the box.* Right. Present first and then sex. The box wasn't taped up so she lifted the lid easily, but whatever was inside was wrapped in bubble wrap. She lifted a piece out and dropped it on the table.

'Oh wait,' Rob said. 'You'll probably need to lift it out.'

Piper reached her hands inside the box and felt something round. She lifted it and Rob pulled the box out of the way, dropping it on the floor. The thing was quite heavy and she rested it on the table as she stripped away the remaining bubble wrap to reveal a glitter ball. She laughed out loud.

'It's electric,' Rob said. 'You can put it on the ceiling or have it standing on your desk or whatever.'

'I love it,' she said.

'It's home-made. Well, school-made. I set it as a project for the boys at school. Some of the boys who left comments. The one who made the photo edit. They really did not enjoy cutting all those tiny squares to my specifications, I can tell you.'

'Oh my god,' Piper said. 'Seriously?'

'Yep. Plus while they were doing it, I showed them Chimamanda Ngozi Adiche's 'We Should All Be Feminists' TED talk on the whiteboard.'

'You did not,' Piper said.

'I did. A couple of them apologised. I know it's you they should be apologising to, not me, but I didn't think you'd actually want to hear from any of the little sods, so…'

'This is amazing,' Piper said. She stared down at the glitter ball, seeing tiny versions of herself reflected over and over and over. 'I love it.'

Rob stepped closer, hooking his chin over her shoulder, his arms sliding around her waist. She gasped as he squeezed. She could see tiny reflections of the two of them now. They were both smiling.

'Why don't you move here?' Piper said before she could change her mind.

'Okay,' Rob said, kissing behind her ear.

'Just like that?'

'Why not?'

Piper turned in his arms to look at him. 'What about your job?'

Rob furrowed his brow, pretending to think. 'I'm fairly sure there are schools in London. Grange Hill? That was in London, wasn't it? Waterloo Road?'

'That's in Rochdale.'

'Is it? Okay, then whatever school William and Kate's kids go to. Or I bet there are even other schools, not frequented by royalty.'

'You think you're clever, don't you?' She bit lightly at his jaw. She loved how his skin tasted.

He smiled, smugly. 'Well I am a teacher.'

Piper rolled her eyes. 'It's a big move. You've got a flat. Friends. Family.'

'They'll all still be there. Even the flat. I could sublet it. And I was thinking it was time for a new challenge anyway.'

'Really?'

'Yes. I've been there a few years now. Plus after what happened on Facebook I've started to think of the students as a bunch of bastards, so a change is probably overdue.'

'Right,' Piper said. 'Okay. I mean, if you were thinking about it anyway...'

He leaned forward, resting his forehead against hers. 'Oh, make no mistake, it wouldn't be because I wanted a change.'

'No?'

'Nope. It would be because I want to be with you.'

'Rob—'

'No, listen. No pressure. Honestly. If you decide you don't want this, if it's too much or too soon or both, then tell me. And we can carry on with long distance. It's not that far. But if we can have more, I want more. I want to wake up with you in the morning. I want to fall asleep with you at night. I want to watch TV with you and eat brunch with you and shower with you and sit in your tiny garden drinking coffee with you. I want to get to know your friends and see London through your eyes and be, you know, together.'

Piper wasn't sure she was breathing. Dots were starting to appear in front of her eyes.

'Also,' Rob said. 'I want to be naked with you. Like, all the time.'

'Okay,' Piper said. 'We can do that. I can do that.'

'Want to start now?' Rob asked.

So they did.

A LETTER FROM KERIS

I want to say a huge thank you for choosing to read *The One that Got Away*. If you did enjoy it, and want to keep up to date with all my latest releases, just sign up at the following link. Your email address will never be shared and you can unsubscribe at any time.

www.bookouture.com/keris-stainton

I hope you loved *The One that Got Away* and if you did I would be very grateful if you could write a review. I'd love to hear what you think, and it makes such a difference helping new readers to discover one of my books for the first time.

I love hearing from my readers – you can get in touch on my Facebook page, through Twitter, Goodreads or my website.

Thanks,
Keris

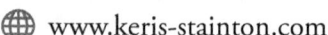 www.keris-stainton.com

 facebook.com/keriswritesbooks

 twitter.com/Keris

ACKNOWLEDGEMENTS

Enormous thanks as always to my fabulous agent, Hannah Sheppard; my amazing editor Abigail Fenton, who always gets what I'm going for, takes no shit, and buys me cake; and everyone at Bookouture who make writing these books so much fun.

Thank you to everyone in The Place and the One Direction Adult Lady Slack who suggested bad (and good) band names, and a massive glass of wine for Alice Broadway who came up with the absolutely perfect 'Bitter/Sweet'.

To all the body positivity and fat acceptance bloggers and Instagrammers who have genuinely changed the way I feel about my body, particularly Body Posi Panda, Becky Barnes and Bethany Rutter.

To all my amazing friends who were so incredibly lovely and supportive when the thing that inspired this book happened. (Everything is copy.)

To Sue Morgan (née Pritchard) and Susan Walters for making my own rubbish teens much more fun, to Lindsay Bown for super-yacht adventures, to Chloe Smith for naming Infinite Plays, and to Frances Jacks for medical advice (obviously any errors are my own).

To everyone at Weatherhead in the 80s and London Records in the mid-90s. All the good bits are based on you, the bad bits I made up. Special shout out to Juliette who thought I'd be amazing in Press – I'll always wish I'd been brave enough.

Finally, as always, to my shipmates, David, Harry and Joe.